IKE
and MAMA
and the
SEVEN
SURPRISES

IKE
and MAMA
and the
SEVEN
SURPRISES

by Carol Snyder
drawings by Charles Robinson

LOTHROP, LEE & SHEPARD BOOKS

NEW YORK

Library of Congress Cataloging in Publication Data

Snyder, Carol.
Ike and Mama and the seven surprises.

Summary: Ike is very skeptical when his mother promises that he will have seven surprises in the month before his Bar Mitzvah, especially with his father still hospitalized with tuberculosis and a newly arrived, jobless cousin living in their small apartment.

1. Children's stories, American. [1. Mothers and sons—Fiction. 2. Jews—Fiction. 3. New York (N.Y.)— Fiction. 4. Family life—Fiction] I. Robinson, Charles, date   , ill. II. Title.
PZ7.S68517Iml 1985   [Fic]   84-17077
ISBN 0-688-03732-1

*Dedicated to the strength of families
and to the memory of my father
Irving Glasberg,
who was proof that "Ike" grew up to be
a hardworking, honest, generous, and successful man
who, having touched many lives, will be
remembered always.*

*With special thanks to my daughter Linda
for her support and excellent typing.*

CONTENTS

1

IKE IN A HURRY

Ike was racing from Public School 43 to Hebrew school when he saw the tiny puppy with its paw caught in the trolley track. Off in the distance he saw the St. Anne's Avenue trolley car coming nearer and nearer, faster and faster. Above the loud clangs of the trolley, the puppy squealed and, without thinking of any danger to himself, Ike dropped his books, ran to the brown puppy and freed its paw from the grooved track. Just in time, Ike snatched him up.

He clutched the puppy to his chest, their two hearts pounding as they escaped from the passing trolley car. As the trolley clacked by, the driver pointed his finger at Ike and scolded him. But the puppy licked Ike right on the mouth.

"You okay now, boy?" Ike asked, putting the puppy down on the sidewalk. "Can you walk? Whose puppy are you? You don't have a collar around your neck."

The tiny puppy tilted its head to one side, stared at Ike, wagged its tail, and barked.

Ike wanted to take the puppy home, but with barely enough food to go around, this September of 1921, Mama would not be happy to have another mouth to feed. Ike picked up his books. "You better go home now," he said to the puppy and started to walk down the block toward cheder, the Hebrew school in the basement classroom of the synagogue. The rabbi would already be there with the seven

other boys preparing for their Bar Mitzvah—their entrance into Jewish manhood. But the puppy showed no intention of leaving him. If Ike took two steps forward so did the brown puppy.

Ike raced ahead, till he tripped and stopped to regain his balance. The puppy raced at his heels breathlessly. Ike laughed as the puppy tripped over paws too big for his tiny body. Nowadays Ike felt as clumsy as this puppy, for his own legs had grown suddenly, and he too tripped more than ever before.

"Go home, boy," he said again. "Your family must be waiting for you." But the puppy followed Ike all the way to cheder on East 146th Street and Brook Avenue.

Ike had to shut the door quickly or the puppy would have followed him right to his seat on the hard wooden bench. From the front of the small, damp room, the rabbi stroked the bottom of his beard as he explained to Ike and the seven other boys seated before him about how each of them would soon be a Bar Mitzvah —a son of the commandments.

"You will be legally responsible for carrying out the commandments of Judaism—the mitzvot—and obligated to do so. You will be legally responsible for your own actions. And before morning prayer you will bind on your left arm and middle of your forehead tefillin—two long, thin leather straps with a small, square, black leather box on each that contains scriptural passages." The rabbi spoke very seriously but Ike could think only of the puppy.

Once he thought he heard it scratching at the wooden door. He looked around the room but no one else seemed to notice. Ike was not the first of his friends to be a Bar Mitzvah. This year alone he'd already been to Morton Weinstein's ceremony and to Cousin Sammy's. Ike's Bar Mitzvah would be next, only a month and a week away, on November third, when he would be thirteen.

The rabbi went on, "You will also, as legal Jewish men, now take on the privileges as well as the responsibilities. You will now be able to have an aliyah, which means coming up to chant the blessing for the Torah reading. The

Bar Mitzvah will demonstrate his knowledge with the Hebrew reading of the Torah, which you have all been studying over the past year. You should all be studying with your papas as well as with me."

With those words, Ike even forgot about the puppy. For a month already Papa had been in the hospital and Ike was so worried about him and missed him so much. Now, with the rabbi's words, he felt an added worry. How would he be ready for his Bar Mitzvah without having Papa to chant and practice with, the way he'd been doing before Papa got tuberculosis? Then, the worst thought yet crossed Ike's mind. What if Papa wasn't well enough to come to his Bar Mitzvah ceremony—wasn't even able to have an aliyah? Ike desperately wished that Papa would be there.

The rabbi's voice vibrated with strength and knowledge as he spoke, looking from boy to boy, soon to be men. "Who will be the first now to read his Torah portion?"

Ike's friend, Herbie Freidman, volunteered and stumbled over the Hebrew words only now and then. Ike shuddered at the thought of the stumbling that he would do.

Then the rabbi went on to discuss the commandment of Bikkur Cholim—visiting the sick. "When one fulfills a commandment—a mitzvah—" the rabbi explained, "one is doing a good deed." The rabbi taught some more about mitzvot. Ike listened, then thought again of Papa.

Ike wanted to visit Papa but so far he'd been forbidden to do so, for fear of catching the disease. But, Ike suddenly thought, to visit the sick is a commandment. He felt confused. His thoughts were interrupted by a yelping sound at the door. But it was when the yelping stopped that he got worried. He found himself hoping the puppy had not gone away.

Today, Hebrew school seemed extra long to Ike, who counted the minutes till it was over. Ike was the first one out of Hebrew school. He was out the door before the other boys had even closed up their books. He looked up and down the block, but he didn't see the puppy. A sad feeling inched through him and he broke into a run as if to escape from it.

This time he tripped, not over his own big

feet, but over the puppy, who, at the sound of Ike's footsteps, had raced after him and cut him off.

Ike bent down and scratched a round circle of white fur on the top of the puppy's head. The puppy's long tongue reached out to lick him. Then the two of them dashed off together.

Ike decided to stop at the butcher shop to see if he could get a scrap of something for the puppy to eat. He stepped over the one-eyed cat sleeping in a sunny spot on the sawdust-covered floor. At Ike's direction the butcher looked out the shop window at the shaggy puppy straining to look in at him with dark, sad eyes. The butcher took out brown paper and wrapped up some cow innards he called "lung and miltz" that he said he was about to throw out. He handed Ike the small package. Outside again, Ike heard his name being shouted from next door.

"Ike! Ike Greenberg!" bellowed Mrs. Miller, the candy store lady, as if he were a mile away. She wiped her hands on her ice-cream-and soda-stained apron. Ike walked to the candy store doorway, where the bell continued tinkling long after the door had been opened. "Quick! Go get your mama," Mrs. Miller ordered, pointing up East 136th Street, to Ike's apartment. "There's a telephone call and it's for her. It's so important the person is holding on. Hurry!"

"Okay, Mrs. Miller. I'll get her!"

Ike started to run. A phone call! He thought as he ran clutching the package the butcher had given him. On East 136th Street in the Bronx, the only phone in the neighborhood was in the corner candy store. Sometimes Ike even earned two cents as a runner and deliverer of phone messages. But this was the first time the phone call was for *his* mama! And important yet!

Ike slid to a halt, suddenly remembering the puppy. He turned around. Sure enough, ears flapping, tongue hanging out of its mouth, panting and heaving to capture a breath, the puppy was dashing after him. "Here boy!" he said, bending down. The puppy leaped into his arms and lapped at his cheeks and ears. He

17

couldn't just leave a puppy whose life he had saved. Together they raced the last half of the block to Ike's stoop.

Ike's friends Danny Mantussi, Tony Golida, Morton Weinstein, James Higgins, Joey, and the three Murphy brothers were crowding around the stoop. And at a nearby patch of dirt surrounding the fire hydrant at the curb, Ike's cousins, Sammy, Dave, Bernie, and Sol were playing mumblety peg, snapping the penknife into the soft dirt square and dividing up the territory.

With the phone call and all, Ike figured now was not the time to tell Mama about the puppy, not just yet. So he handed the round, wriggly bundle of fur to Morton saying, "Hold this and don't tell anyone about him. I gotta get my mama, she's got a phone call."

"A phone call!" The boys shouted as they watched Ike dash up the stairs. Then Sammy and Dave and tall Danny Mantussi raced after him to find out more about this event.

Ike took two steps at a time and, breathless, bounded in the doorway of his third floor apartment. "Mrs. Miller said . . . " He tried to shout out the news but Mama shushed him without listening.

"Oy, Ikey. Shah. Mrs. Weinstein and Rosie are here with Baby Murray. Don't scare the little one. Oy, do I love babies," Mama crooned as she rocked the flannel bundle. "And close the door, Ikey, cats come up."

Ike's sister, Bessie, tugged at Mama's skirt wanting her to bend down to give a better view of the baby.

"A phone call," Ike yelled, prompted by Sammy, Dave, and Danny who crowded behind Ike in the doorway.

"Oh, for me? It must be Arnold." Rosie, Mrs. Weinstein's daughter, living uptown with her husband Arnold, was used to the telephone.

"It's not for you, Rosie."

"So who is it for, me?" Mrs. Weinstein muttered. "Who calls me except Rosie and she's here. Tell already, Ikey. Before he tells something, you could plotz—fall apart, explode —from this child," she explained the Yiddish word to Danny Mantussi.

"*Puvulya,*" Mama said and patted the air with her hand in a calming motion.

Papa's word for "relax," Ike thought. *Papa always says puvulya when he wants you to slow down.* The thought of Papa brought a wrinkle of worry to Ike's brow. "The phone call's for you, Mama. And it's important. Mrs. Miller said the person is holding on."

"Holding on? What are we waiting for?" Rosie grabbed the baby and Mama practically flew out the doorway. Lifting the bottom of her long black skirt, she started down the stairs, huffing and puffing more at each landing. Ike raced after her.

Mrs. Weinstein, Rosie clutching the baby, and Bessie followed. Down the stoop they all went, passing Morton and the other boys who hid the puppy. Down the block to the corner candy store they trooped. The doorbell jingled the announcement of Mama's arrival.

Mrs. Miller handed Mama the receiver that hung from the wall and everyone barely breathed as they listened and waited. Inside the store, good smells and memories of cool lime rickey drinks; foaming egg creams of seltzer, milk, and chocolate; licorice sticks; and rolls of button candies made Ike's mouth water.

First, all Mama said was "Hello, hello! Hello, hello!" and then turning to Mrs. Miller added, "Why is this phone making spitting noises?"

"It's the connection," Mrs. Miller said. "Just talk anyway."

Then all Mama said was "Yes" and "I see" and "Yes" and "I see" and "Goodbye."

"So who is it, already?" Mrs. Weinstein was the first to ask. "You could plotz from this waiting. It is bad news?"

"Oy," said Mama, and her mouth hung open and she slapped her own cheek. "Thank God it was not a call to tell me Papa is worse. No. It is good news just at a bad time. Someone none of you know, a little someone, is coming to live with us," Mama said very seriously, as if trying to get used to the idea, herself.

A little someone? Was that like a little stranger? Ike thought, remembering that when Rosie was having Baby Murray, she'd announced to people that she was having a little stranger. "That's what they say uptown," she'd explained, "uptown on the Concourse." But Mama? . . .

"So tell already, Mama," Ike finally spoke. "You are going to have a baby?"

"A what?" Mama said.

"A baby," Ike repeated, scratching his head.

Bessie tugged on Mama's skirt. "Who is having a baby?"

"I don't know. Who? I give up." Mama answered as if it was one more of Bessie's second grade riddles.

Ike could hardly stand the suspense a moment longer. "The phone call, Mama. You said a little someone was coming to live with us. Isn't that like a little stranger? Doesn't that mean that you're having a baby? A little while ago, when you held Baby Murray, you even said how much you love babies."

"Oy, Ikey." Mama's face turned almost as red as Ike's as she pinched his cheeks and chuckled.

Ike tried to wriggle out of her clutches. He

was almost thirteen and not sure he liked hugs anymore—not from Mama, anyway—at least not in front of everyone.

"Mama isn't having a baby," she said, explaining the phone call. "You, Bessie, and I are all going to have a little someone none of you know come to live with us. And his name is Cousin Jake. He is a fine grown-up man who just did not grow to be very tall. He is my cousin, my Aunt Chava's son, just arrived from Russia. And it will be good, Ikey, to have a man around the house, a learned man who knows Torah and can help you prepare for your Bar Mitzvah."

Green ones, greena couzinas, the newcomers were teasingly called, Ike thought, as if they were unripened fruit, not ready for America. Just ready to give you a good bellyache if you took one in. It was Papa Ike longed to have help him study, not some stranger. And with Cousin Jake around, Mama would no longer consider Ike to be the man of the house. She would no longer ask Ike about business decisions or let him say the morning prayers.

Cousin Jake would do all that now. And would Bessie still come to him for advice? These were the worries that tripped over each other in Ike's mind.

"On the phone was the man from the Hebrew Immigrant Aid Society," Mama continued. "H.I.A.S. he calls it. He was trying to find a relative to take in Cousin Jake."

"And that is you?" Mrs. Weinstein asked. "Another mouth to feed?"

Mama straightened herself up. She was only four feet seven inches and Ike was already much taller. But although she still looked quite small, Mama made herself sound big.

"I have never closed my door to the needy," Mama spoke loudly and clearly. "Especially not family. It will only be for a while till Cousin Jake can live on his own."

Ike took a deep breath. Not because he enjoyed the thought of a greena couzina living with them—probably sleeping in his bed, eating his and Bessie's food, even acting odd in front of his friends, like the cousin that once stayed at his friend Herbie's house. But because he had an idea—and a problem of his own to solve.

"Mama, you mean that you never turn the needy away from your home?"

"Of course I mean it, Ikey. It is a mitzvah, a commandment to take care of a needy being."

"Good," said Ike. "Then you won't be mad at me."

"What did you do now, Ikey, dear?" Mama spoke sweetly but raised one eyebrow which meant possible Mama trouble.

"I too have done a mitzvah today," Ike explained. "And right now it is waiting by the stoop."

"What are you talking, Ikey?" Mama said. "Riddles like Bessie?" And she sank down onto a nearby wooden chair.

"No, Mama," Ike answered. "I too have brought home a little stranger to live with us."

With these words Ike led Mama out of the candy store and up the block past the butcher, the grocery store, and the Chinese laundry. Bessie, Mrs. Weinstein, and Rosie carrying Baby Murray, followed.

At the stoop, the East 136th Street army of boys was gathered. When they saw Ike give the okay sign, they stepped aside revealing the wiggling, licking, needy being they'd been hiding.

"Here boy! Good boy!" Ike knelt down and let the brown furry puppy cover his face with puppy kisses.

"Whose cute little puppy?" Mama, with great effort and groaning, bent down, cooed, and stroked the puppy's velvety soft, but dirty, head and ears.

"Our puppy," Ike answered.

"You mean my puppy, too, Ikey?" Bessie begged.

"Your puppy, too," Ike said, giving in to make Bessie happy, as he often did.

"It cannot be our puppy, Ikey dear." Mama said. "There is not even enough food for people these days no less dogs. How are we going to feed a puppy? We already have Cousin Jake to feed now."

"But, Mama," Ike started to speak.

"No 'But Mama's,' " Mama answered.

Ike continued his pleading, anyway. "I

have already made arrangements. I stopped at
the butcher and he gave me the cow innards for
free and he said I could have more whenever I
needed to feed Boy."

"Who is Boy?" Mama asked, still confused
with all the excitement.

"Boy is my dog . . . our dog," Ike said
hopefully.

"Again with the riddles?" Mama groaned.

"His name must be Boy," Ike went on,
"because whenever I call, 'Here Boy,' he looks
up and runs to me. He followed me home from
Hebrew school today, after I saved his life," Ike
explained.

"You what?" Mama asked.

"He looks very needy, Mama, right? He
was almost hit by the St. Anne's Avenue trolley, as I was on my way home from school.
Right in front of my eyes I saw the trolley
coming and I pulled the puppy away just in
time. I saved his life."

"Only a boy, and you have saved a life,"
Mama said, respectfully looking upward as if to
be sure God was hearing all this. Then she

looked back at Ike and added, "That means you will have seven surprises before sundown on the day you are a man. Some you will get and some you will give. Most will be good, maybe all if you are ready to think like a man. My mama's mama in Russia once said that."

Seven surprises in only a month and a week? Ike thought with disbelief. Would he think like a man in time for his Bar Mitzvah? He wasn't even sure he would be able to chant the blessings well, no less think like a man. Many times Ike even forgot to think before he acted.

"But oy, Ikey." Mama then sighed and clutched at her heart. "With the trolley coming you went by the tracks? You could have been hurt."

"Nah," Ike said. "I was careful."

"So," said Mama, looking up at the sky, her way of talking to God. "You are sending special delivery to the Greenberg family today? You are having, maybe, a special on mitzvahs? Well, who am I to say no to one greena couzina and one poor little puppy, if you were good enough to save my Ikey from being hurt by the trolley car. Thank you, God. And now if I could be so bold as to ask something of you. If you could just make Papa well again, maybe in time for Ike's Bar Mitzvah, we would be so grateful."

2
WORRIES

Mama's words filled Ike with thoughts of Papa. Thoughts so important they blocked out the street noises of a passing horse-drawn tar-wagon. They even blocked out the chattering of the East 136th Street army of boys hoping that the wagon would stop so they could get some tar to chew. He didn't hear Baby Murray hiccuping in Rosie's arms or Mrs.

Weinstein saying "Boo!" to scare the hiccups away. Ike didn't even hear the puppy squeal when he hugged him a little too tightly. He was so deep in thoughts about Papa.

It was already a month since Papa had been too sick with coughing to work as a pants presser in the clothing factory. The doctors at Bellevue Hospital had told Mama that Papa had a lung sickness. TB everyone called it. Ike missed Papa so much that it was like an ache. Some mornings he'd go to Papa's soft parlor chair with the rip in it. He would rub his cheek against the spot that still smelled like Papa's hair cream. Ike missed feeling Papa's strong hand on his shoulder after they'd prayed together. He missed Papa's laugh when he said something funny. He missed Papa's understanding words said when Ike's voice changed octave without warning. "You are growing up," Papa would say. "Your voice is also growing. That is good." And he even missed Papa's scolding him when he was late for dinner, and his complaining that he ate too much, too fast. Ike whispered in Boy's ear, "Now, when

31

there's so much to say, I wish at least I could talk to Papa. And I wish more than anything that Papa could get well in time to be at my Bar Mitzvah." Impossible, he thought, but kept on wishing.

If Papa had been in nearby Lincoln Hospital for the past month, it would be easy to see him. But for tuberculosis, Papa had to rest in Bellevue Hospital at the East River in Manhattan. He had to be near the Floating Hospital Ship of St. John's Guild, which took him for day-trips to clear his lungs with fresh sea air. One of these days, Mama said, she would take Ike with her to visit him—when the doctor said it was okay.

This afternoon, in cheder, the rabbi had talked to the boys about the importance of carrying out the commandments—the mitzvot. "As many as possible or with great significance," he'd said. "Especially with your Bar Mitzvahs so near. There are 613 mitzvot listed in the Bible," he'd instructed. Ike had thought and thought. He knew he wanted to do a mitzvah for Papa. But what?

Mama had said it was a blessing that there had been room enough for Papa on the hospital ship. So many people were sick with TB. To Ike it didn't seem like a blessing. It just seemed far away. Ike wasn't sure he could wait much longer to speak to Papa. He needed him now. He wanted to tell him about Boy the dog, about the way one ear stands straight up and the other flips over when he hears Ike's voice. And about the way his tail wags in a circle when he's happy. He needed Papa to hear him practice for his Bar Mitzvah, just a month and a week away. He needed to hear Papa say, "That was good, Ikey." Or, "Do it again like this." But most of all he needed Papa . . . just because he was Papa.

Ike was startled back to the present when Boy licked him right on the mouth, and Mama said, "Feh! Ikey, not on the mouth." And she reached over and took Boy out of Ike's arms and spoke to him, explaining, "If you like to smell garbage in the street and whatnot, you don't lick on the mouth. You understand, Boy-chik?" Everyone listened to Mama, shopkeepers, teachers, and principals, the East 136th Street army of boys crowding the stoop, Mrs. Weinstein and Rosie, even Boy stared at her as if he understood every word. Until Mama said, "Good!" Then Boy licked her right on the mouth. "Feh!" Mama said, handing Boy back to Ike.

"Feh!" Mrs. Weinstein said. "Rosie, keep the baby away from that dirty dog," she added.

"Now," Mama said, "we have got things to do to get ready for Cousin Jake."

Ike got a worried feeling just thinking about Cousin Jake.

"They are bringing him in a horse-drawn wagon all the way from the H.I.A.S. building on Lafayette Place in New York. Imagine what nice people to save me a trip. And what a trip Cousin Jake has had already. So many days in steerage on the boat. And for weeks he's been on Ellis Island being questioned and checked by doctors till the H.I.A.S. man picked him up there and found me. Oy, Minnie, you and I remember. Weeks like that you never forget." Mama reminded Mrs. Weinstein of their own

passage from Russia. Then Mama switched her voice from sad to merry.

"So if I remember Cousin Jake, what he likes best to eat is kreplach. So kreplach he must have waiting for him special after his long voyage."

"Um, kreplach," Ike's cousin Dave said, and Bernie licked his lips. "Kreplach is a Yiddish word for meat inside a jacket of dough," he explained to Tony Golida. "And Ike's Mama makes it the best."

"The greena couzina will probably eat all the food up so fast you won't even get to taste it, Ike," Sammy said. "That's what happened when we had a greena uncle stay with us once." With these words, the worried feeling in Ike's stomach grew.

"Kreplach you're going to make now?" Mrs. Weinstein said. "With what are you going to stuff the dough? Dollar bills are falling from the sky?"

"I'll find something," Mama said. "If you look . . . you find."

"Wait a minute," Mrs. Weinstein said, "I

just remembered. I have from yesterday some leftover meat that Rosie brought me. So come. We'll get it." Mrs. Weinstein muttered, "She goes and takes in a boarder yet."

"I am not taking in a boarder," Mama said. "I am taking in family in need and that is a pleasure."

Then they started up the steps of the stoop. "Wait on the corner for the wagon from H.I.A.S.," Mama said to Ike, "so you'll show them the way. Bessie, come with me so you'll help me pinch the dough." With the others gone, Ike gathered his friends and cousins around him.

"We had a relative come from the other side," Tony Golida said. "He was always breaking things and making a flood in the bathroom. You'll see, Ikey. You'll have to clean up after him."

"Yeah, Ike. They get you into trouble," Danny added.

"And you'll probably have to teach him English, too, instead of playing mumblety peg."

After each bit of information from his helpful friends, Ike worried some more. He just knew he was not going to like Cousin Jake. He wished Papa was here. Papa should be told the news about Cousin Jake. Maybe he wouldn't like him moving in. If only he could speak to Papa. Ike had to think of something—a way to get to Papa. But how?

"Now we better get over to Miller's Candy Store," Ike said. "We gotta watch for my Cousin Jake, from Russia."

"How ya gonna know it's him?" Tony asked.

"I'll just know," Ike said, " 'cause he's family."

The army trudged up the block and, to Mrs. Miller's dismay, draped themselves over the chained-down newspaper stand in front of her corner store. The two bricks and a wire that held down the stacks of newspapers soon became an instrument on which Danny Mantussi strummed a slightly ragtime beat yelling, "Guess what song?"

" 'How Ya Gonna Keep 'Em Down on the Farm After They've Seen Paree,' " guessed

Sammy, snapping the elastic on his suspenders in time to the beat.

"Nah, you're wrong," said Danny. "What are you, tone deaf? Can't you tell it's 'The Charleston'?" Then he strummed what he said was a different tune—but Ike thought it sounded exactly the same.

Ike was glancing at the headlines on the *Journal American*, something about prohibition and the gangster, Meyer Lansky, when Mrs. Miller came charging out of her store shooing the boys away with her apron as if they were chickens. So Ike led the boys away from the newsstand and started to teach Boy some tricks to pass the time as they waited and waited for the delivery of Cousin Jake.

"Sit, Boy," Ike said, and started to add, "and stay . . ." but Boy rolled over begging to have his stomach rubbed. So Ike quickly changed his command to, "Roll over," and declared how smart Boy was.

Dave tickled Boy's stomach and gave him a push. "Roll over, Boy. Good Boy. See, he really is smart," Dave agreed.

Ike kept looking at any horse-drawn

wagon that passed by. But none that he saw looked like it was carrying one greena couzina named Jake. What if Jake was mean? Ike worried. What if he took over Papa's place, sat in Papa's special chair with the rip in it? Ike wasn't sure he'd like all these changes.

Ike picked up Boy and kissed his fuzzy head. At least Boy would listen to him and obey his orders. He put the dog down. "Roll over," he commanded. But Boy just sat down, wagged his tail in a circle, and blinked his eyes. Then he backed up, jumped high up into Ike's arms and licked him on the mouth.

As Ike turned his head to escape another lick, he spotted the horse-drawn tar-wagon that had passed by earlier. The men who'd been on it were fixing the road just around the corner. He could already smell the hot tar. "C'mon," he shouted to the others. "Let's get some tar to chew."

"What if you miss the wagon with yer Cousin Jake?" Morton asked.

But they were on their way and soon were close enough to feel the heat of the furnace on the tar-wagon, yet not too close to be seen by the workers. The workmen were busy splitting a barrel in half, then chopping up some hard black pitch that looked like a mirror on the inside. They left it heating in the furnace and went to set up wooden blocks in the street. When the tar was melted, Ike knew they'd take tar from a bucket with a long-handled dipper and, if the boys were lucky, the tar would drip on the side of the wagon.

Sure enough, as the men went back to fix the road, a long drip of the hot, clean, pure tar hardened on the wagon and the boys lifted it off like a candle dripping. They bit and pulled at it like taffy, and chewed on it like gum, enjoying the gasoline taste. Ike busily molded the tar on his front teeth to look like he was toothless. One by one the boys mimicked Ike and put tar on their teeth and smiled. They were making each other laugh when a horse-drawn wagon carrying a strange-looking passenger approached. The horse and wagon stopped, then moved forward and stopped again. The horse whinnied and swished its tail.

"You lookin' for the Greenbergs of East 136th Street?" Morton Weinstein called. Since he'd turned thirteen last month and already had his Bar Mitzvah ceremony, he'd become more serious. Even now, he'd been keeping watch while the others were fooling around.

The wagon came to a halt and a man wearing a real straw hat said, "Yes, we are looking for the Greenbergs. Can you direct us?"

Ike looked past the nicely dressed man to the passenger, a little man who sat twirling his side curls around his crooked finger. The man wore a black hat, had a heavy black beard, and a shirt with a high collar. And on his lap was a huge bundle. A rolled up perrina, the biggest feather quilt Ike had ever seen. It had little holes all over it. Ike thought the black-edged holes looked like they'd been burnt into the quilt. He wondered why Jake carried bedding with him.

Ike motioned the driver to follow him to his house. Then he looked into Cousin Jake's eyes to check for meanness. But instead he saw the makings of a tear. And Jake reached out toward the sidewalk for Ike's hand as if knowing he was family.

Ike reached upward and smiled, forgetting he'd blacked out his teeth with tar. So did the other boys—all looking toothless. Cousin Jake, wide-eyed with fright, pointed his finger at the strange-looking boys. Before he was aware of what was happening, Boy reached his head upward and bit Cousin Jake's extended finger!

3
MAMA AND COUSIN JAKE IN ACTION

"Oy yoy!" Cousin Jake yelped in Yiddish instead of saying hello in English. His eyes opened wide again and he shuddered.

Ike couldn't believe Boy had bitten Jake's finger. Ike checked it. Luckily the skin wasn't broken. He had started to apologize for Boy, and at the same time introduce himself, but only managed to mumble, "Cousin Jake, I am

Ike Greenberg and . . ." before having to stop to unstick his tar-covered teeth. By then the wagon carrying the greena couzina was moving down the street to the clopping sounds of the horse's hooves. Jake wouldn't have understood English anyway, Ike figured.

Ike ripped the tar off his teeth and threw it in the gutter. Then with a tap on Boy's nose, the words, "Bad Boy," and a wave to his friends to follow him, Ike ran to catch up with his terrified older cousin.

The wagon came to a halt in front of Ike's house. He peered up at his bearded cousin perched up on the wagon seat. Ike offered to carry Jake's bundles, but when Ike started to take them, Jake pulled away. He did this whenever Ike and Boy came near him. Once, Boy even sniffed at Jake and growled. Ike wondered if Boy could smell Jake's fear, or was he sniffing at the goose-down perrina—the huge comforter with the burn holes—that Cousin Jake clutched? Ike couldn't help wondering how all those burn holes got there. And why was Jake clutching at the perrina, anyway?

He walked over to the driver's side. "My name is Ike Greenberg," he announced to the well-dressed man from H.I.A.S. "And I live on the third floor front. Follow me." Ike raced up the steps two at a time. So did the other boys. He wondered if Jake would think that in America you must walk up stairs that way. Ike turned to look at Jake and noticed that he had a slight limp.

Mrs. Mantussi stuck her head out the doorway of her apartment on the second floor as the boys passed by. "Always in a hurry these children," she muttered.

As he reached the door to his apartment, Ike opened it. Before entering, he waited a minute for Jake and the man from H.I.A.S. to catch their breath. He heard Mama yelling at Bessie.

"How can I make kreplach, Bessie darling," Mama said, "if you are nibbling all the meat filling? Puvulya. Relax. You will have plenty when they are cooked."

"But it's so good, Mama," Bessie said, licking a speck of meat from her lips.

"And you are hungry for meat, aren't you? Oy, Papa," Mama moaned. "It is not easy with you sick and away."

"We are here," Ike said loudly. "The man from H.I.A.S., me, Boy, Cousin Jake, and everyone!"

Mama came out of the kitchen wiping her hands on her checked apron. Out of all the faces she picked just one. "Jake," she said with a catch in her voice. "Oy, Jake. You made it." And she put both her hands on Jake's cheeks and looked into his eyes. And he put both his hands on her cheeks and looked into her eyes.

The apartment smelled good. Boy's nose twitched this way and that searching out the fried meat and onion smells. So did Ike's. The boys all crowded in the apartment to catch another look at Jake. They had seen other newly arrived immigrants in the neighborhood with strange baggy suits and foreign-looking caps, long beards and side curls. But Jake was so short and on his back was pinned a paper that had the letter L on it.

"I see you are curious about the letter L."

Mama explained, "At Ellis Island, where people enter this country, doctors examine them and pin a letter L if they limp or H if their hearts pound. Cousin Jake was born with one leg shorter than the other. He has always limped." Then she added, "Better go now, boys. We have family business. And, Danny dear, close the door on your way out. Cats come up."

The East 136th Street army instantly obeyed and left. Everyone listened to Mama. That is, except Boy, the dog. When Mama came near him, he reached his head out as far as he could from Ike's arms and licked Mama right on the lips. "Feh! Don't do that, Boychik," she sighed. But he did it again all the same.

Cousin Jake pulled back and shuddered.

"Don't worry, Jake," Mama soothed in Yiddish, but Ike understood her words. "This is a lovely little puppy. Not like the fearful dogs in Russia sent to chase us. This dog, Boychik, wouldn't harm even a flea."

But Cousin Jake knew better. He rubbed his sore finger.

"Sit down, gentlemen," Mama said to Jake and the man from H.I.A.S. "You are hungry maybe? Ikey, go bring some fruit out in a bowl and put on the kitchen floor a dish of milk for Boy."

Speaking in Yiddish so Cousin Jake would understand, the man from H.I.A.S. asked Mama to sign some papers, and by the time Ike returned from the kitchen with the bowl of fruit, the man had left. Ike was not happy to find Cousin Jake seated comfortably in Papa's special chair with the rip. It gave him a wiggly feeling in his stomach.

Ike stepped into the parlor and placed the bowl of fruit on the little table next to Jake. Jake looked around the floor of the room.

"The puppy is in the kitchen," Mama explained in Yiddish.

Jake sighed with relief.

"Go ahead, Jake. Eat something." Mama pointed to the crockery fruit bowl. When he still hesitated, Mama took a perfectly ripened banana and handed it to him. "You are in America now, not in steerage on the ship. No

need to look hungrily." She took the big perrina he clutched and put it under the table,
explaining, "It's the one thing he owns. It's the
only reminder of his homeland. That is why he
clings to the quilt." Ike and Bessie stared at the
greena couzina. Ike couldn't believe what he
saw next. There was Jake, eating the banana—
skin and all. Bessie burst out laughing at the
sight. Mama stopped fixing a doily that had
fallen from the arm of the chair, and shook
Bessie's shoulders to quiet her. Then she
looked in the direction of Bessie's stare.

After swallowing a bite, Cousin Jake stuttered his first words. And much to everyone's
surprise they were in English.

"Vat a funny tasting piece dis is. Do I talk
good, no? I have fear to speak. But still in
Russia I study and study to learn talking like
America man."

It was then that Mama spoke. "What a
smart man you are Jake to already have learned
some English. That is good. Now I will teach
you something more. I forgot in Russia we had
no bananas. That's the name of this yellow

fruit, but first you must take off the skin like this." Mama reached out and peeled the banana for Cousin Jake.

Jake hit himself on the forehead with the palm of his hand and stuttered slowly. "In new country even smart man of words and books is dope. Is right word, 'dope'? I learn on Ellis Island."

Ike wanted to tell him, "Yes, anyone who comes in and sits right down in Papa's special chair is a dope." But instead he sighed with relief. At least he wouldn't have to teach him English. He'd already decided to have as little to do with him as possible.

"Oy, Jake," Mama crooned. "Dope is not the right word. Smart is the right word for you. So call yourself smart and you will be smart."

Why don't you call yourself gone, Ike thought, *and be gone.*

Then Jake pulled something out of his pocket. He put a cigarette in his mouth, lit it, puffed and coughed. "See," he said, "now I look America, nu?"

"Feh to smoking." Mama fanned the air as

she spoke. "That you don't need to learn. Oy, such a hurry to fit in. I remember that, too. But you will see. Puvulya, relax. It will all work out."

For a moment Ike felt sorry for Jake.

"And," Jake went on, "I say more like America man. When happy, like now, I say, OH BOY! OH BOY! OH BOY!"

With those innocently spoken words, a large furry bullet with a milk-covered chin, shot out of the nearby kitchen, charged, and jumped right into Cousin Jake's lap. The cigarette fell from his mouth, burned a hole in his shirt, then landed on Papa's chair.

"OY YOY! OY GEVALT!" Cousin Jake exclaimed, pushing himself back into Papa's chair as if he could make himself disappear like chicken fat melting into matzoh on passover.

"Quick, Ikey—get some water," Mama screamed as a wisp of smoke started to rise from Papa's chair.

Ike raced to the kitchen sink to get the water. As he looked for a container, he spoke to Bessie who had followed him. "If a glassful is good for saving Papa's chair, a pitcher would be better." So Ike and Bessie went back to the parlor, and when Bessie tried to get in front of Ike, he tripped and dumped a whole pitcherful of water, aiming at the smoldering spot on the chair, but splashing Jake and Boy as well. A straggly Boy looked around angrily, growled, then turned back to his business of eating the banana droppings in Cousin Jake's long beard.

"OY YOY!" Jake sputtered. "Go away, beast! He vants to eat me up!" And he shooed Boy away. So of course Boy nipped his other finger. But only Ike and Bessie saw that. Mama had turned to take the pitcher from Ike. She put it down freeing her hands to grab Boy. She raised an eyebrow indicating Mama trouble.

"Ikey, what is with you? A flood we didn't need." *In trouble already because of Cousin Jake*, Ike thought.

Then Mama cuddled the wet puppy. "Don't worry, Jake," she soothed, trying to calm him and the dog. "Boychik loves you." She stroked Boy's wet, furry head as she talked. "He wouldn't hurt anyone. He is welcoming

you, as we all are welcoming you, to America and to our happy home." At the sound of her voice, Boy turned to Mama and licked her on the lips. "Feh!" she said.

The only thing that calmed Cousin Jake was when Mama found the magic word. "And special for you, Jake, I made your favorite for dinner tonight. Kreplach."

"Kreplach?" Cousin Jake stopped shaking at the mention of his favorite food. He reached out to hold Mama's hand and threw her a kiss of thanks.

Then Mama added the painful words: "You are even here, Jake, in time to help Ike practice for his Bar Mitzvah and to celebrate with us. Poor Papa is sick with tuberculosis in the hospital. He helped Ikey with Hebrew for his Bar Mitzvah Torah reading for one month only before he had to go away. Ikey will need your help . . . and he also can help teach you even more English."

"Sickness?" Jake said. "Oy gevalt!" And he clicked his tongue. Then he smiled and said, "I help Ikey. Yes. I make him do right." And he reached out and put his small hand on Ike's shoulder. "And Ikey help me," Jake added.

Ike shuddered at the touch and at the thought of Cousin Jake making him do anything, taking over not only Papa's chair but also what had become Papa's favorite job—helping Ike with his Bar Mitzvah practice. Ike was sure Papa was the only one smart enough to teach him. Each evening for the month before he got so sick, Papa had chanted to Ike the Torah segment—the beginning of the Noah story— that Ike was to memorize. And Ike also was sure he wouldn't like being Cousin Jake's teacher. *I need you, Papa,* he said to himself.

4
IKE'S SPECIAL PLAN

At dinner that night, Cousin Jake wolfed down the kreplach, barely stopping to chew the meat-filled dough. Mama watched him with a smile of satisfaction on her face. Ike and Bessie watched with disappointment as the plate was emptied faster than they could reach for seconds. And Boy looked on, enviously sniffing the air and yelping, jumping up to see over the rim of the carton in which Mama had confined the tiny puppy.

After dinner Mama ordered Ike to practice his Torah portion with Cousin Jake.

"I don't want to practice with him," Ike said to Mama. But the only response he got from her was a raised eyebrow which meant Mama trouble. So Ike started chanting and Cousin Jake started correcting, sometimes in Russian, sometimes in Yiddish, and sometimes in English, but usually it sounded like a mixture of the three languages. Ike did not understand much of what he said, and what he did understand, he didn't like.

"Talk in a big voice when you talk to God," Cousin Jake said. He would hold his ear to show that he couldn't hear the words Ike was practically whispering into his book. But Ike knew that God could hear even the quiet voice of the tiniest child, so he wasn't worried. And he really didn't care if Cousin Jake heard him chant, or not. Ike hated every minute of this. If he had been chanting with Papa, it would have been a happy time.

To make matters worse Ike felt ignored when Bessie, who usually asked Ike for help, brought Cousin Jake her cigar-box doll carriage to fix. Then after helping Ike and Bessie, Cousin Jake relaxed in Papa's chair. Ike hated the way Jake sat in the chair as if he were born there. As if it were his. Even falling asleep in it with a lit cigarette in his hand.

Ike called Mama into the room and pointed to Jake. Mama was so tired from the busy day that she just yawned and said, "Shah, Ike. He's sleeping. Bring me his perrina."

"But what are we going to do with Jake during the night, Mama?" Ike asked, pointing out the burn holes in the heavy quilt, and the lit cigarette in his hand. "Did you see his perrina? It's full of burn holes."

"Burn holes?" Mama said, and she examined the perrina Ike took from under the table where it had been stored. "You are right, Ike. We will have to do something about the cigarettes."

"Cousin Jake might set the house on fire and not just the chair," Ike added, trying to think of as many things as he could to get Jake out of Papa's chair, out of the house, and out of his life. "Maybe he should sleep outside on the fire escape for tonight and leave tomorrow," Ike suggested.

"No," Mama said. "I will just have to stay up and stand guard over Cousin Jake, like a soldier, to make sure he doesn't smoke during the night." As she spoke she took the lit cigarette into the kitchen and put it out. Then she returned to the parlor. "It's too cool at night to have him sleep on the fire escape," Mama said, then yawned again.

"No, Mama. You go to sleep. I'll stay awake and guard."

"But, Ikey, you have school in the morning. How will you get up?" Mama asked.

"I'll be fine," Ike said. "I'm strong," he added, puffing out his chest and making a muscle bulge by bending his arm.

Mama chuckled. "Okay," she agreed. "You stand guard first but wake me in a couple of hours and I'll take over. And, Ikey, keep a little water by you . . . just in case."

Mama changed the subject by pointing to the carton and getting Ike some old rags to make a bed for Boy. "Keep the box in the kitchen," Mama instructed. "It's only the last week in September, but already it's too cool this evening to give Boy a bath. So just find a brush and brush him good."

Ike found a brush all right, the one Mama had given to Cousin Jake. Mama was in the kitchen and didn't see the brush Ike was using. Boy loved being brushed. He growled when Ike stopped. Ike liked the way Boy's brown fur glistened. He prepared the puppy's bed and placed Boy in the rag-lined carton. In the oven of the big black coal stove Mama heated a brick, then wrapped it in a towel and placed it in the box "To give Boy a warm feeling, like a mama," she explained.

Still in the kitchen, Ike happily looked at the September page on the hanging wall calendar. It was full of red crayon x's. Now Ike made a red x on September twenty-eighth, continuing to mark off the days until November third, the day of his Bar Mitzvah. *If only Papa could be well enough to be with me then,* he thought.

It was a restless night in the Greenberg

apartment. Boy whimpered from the cardboard box bed. Cousin Jake snored and sputtered from his perrina cocoon. Mama had covered him with his feather quilt as he slumbered in Papa's chair. Next to him, Ike was wrapped in his own heavy quilt. He was lying on the floor looking up at Jake. Ike was too tired to stand guard every minute. So occasionally he would doze.

At the sound of the dog, Jake would sit up in terror and, to calm himself, light a cigarette. Ike would hand him the big seashell from Coney Island to use as an ashtray. Cousin Jake would hold the shell, mutter "Vos it?" and put it to his ear not understanding Ike's words as he tried to explain the use of the shell as an ashtray. Ike finally gave up and lay down, after helping Jake put out the cigarette.

Then as Ike dozed, Jake lit another cigarette, puffed, relaxed, and fell asleep. At the smell of smoke and burning goose feathers, Ike sat up in terror, reaching for the pitcher of water Mama had instructed him to keep nearby . . . "in case." He poured some of the water on the smoldering cigarette and the new burn hole in Cousin Jake's goose down perrina, careful not to wet it so much that Jake would awaken and start the scene all over again.

Ike's eyelids alone felt as if they weighed a ton. But his mind was wide awake and spinning thoughts. This had been an exciting and tiring day of surprises. Two so far: Being allowed to keep Boy and Cousin Jake's arrival. Could Mama's grandmother from Russia have been right? He wondered. For saving a life, Ike figured it should be seven *good* surprises before he was a man, and he could think of nothing good about the arrival of Cousin Jake. Ike thought about the words Mama's grandmother from Russia had told her. For the first time he realized she hadn't said the surprises would be good or bad. She had said "Some you will get and some you will give. Most will be good, maybe all if you are ready to think like a man." But what did that mean?

Ike also figured with only a little more than a month till he was a man and five more surprises to make seven, he'd help out in the surprise department and give one to Papa, a good one. But what? It sure would be nice to send with Mama a surprise present for Papa, Ike decided. Something to help him get better faster. Ike thought and thought about surprise number three. What kind of something could make someone feel better? He thought some more.

"Take this. It will make you feel stronger," Mama had once said, giving Ike a spoonful of cod liver oil. Just the thought of that fishy taste made him able to smell it, and in the dark he made a puckered face as if tasting it. He would not send cod liver oil to Papa. He loved him too much to do that.

"This horseradish is so strong, it could cure what ails you," Papa had once said when eating gefilte fish dipped in it. But then Ike remembered Papa had swallowed the piece of seasoned minced fish dipped in horseradish, then gasped and said, "It takes your breath away." No. A gift of horseradish would not make Papa better. He needed to breathe more, not less.

Then it came to Ike. The perfect surprise number three and the perfect mitzvah for Papa. He thought back to something the rabbi had once said about how you must cheer the sick and give them hope. The rabbi called this mitzvah, Bikkur Cholim. He even said how the person who performs this mitzvah would achieve eternal reward. Ike wondered if God had whispered in his ear this gift that might help make Papa feel better faster. Somehow Ike knew that the perfect surprise for Papa, the perfect mitzvah as well, wasn't anything Ike could hand him.

It was something Papa had often said about how just the sight of his family or his neighbors and friends made him feel like a million bucks. Ike figured a million bucks must feel pretty good. And Papa also had encouraged Ike to bring friends home. To let him know they'd be welcomed, Papa would say, "Your friends are my friends." So bringing Papa family and friends, himself and the East 136th Street army of boys, might make Papa feel better. And maybe when you feel better, you get better. That was it. The mitzvah for Papa would be a surprise visit on one of his daily sea-air treatments on the floating hospital ship. They probably wouldn't all be able to get aboard the hospital ship, but Ike could tell everyone to line up on the pier and wave, and Papa could see them from the deck and wave back. And Ike figured why shouldn't his thirteen friends and his dog, Boy, also achieve eternal reward?

Ike just couldn't wait any longer to see for himself how Papa was feeling. Tomorrow he'd tell the others his special plan. This week, as soon as possible, they'd ride to Manhattan—to the floating hospital ship. Ike decided this was such a double good idea that he'd count the hospital visit to Papa as surprise number three, and the present of hope and love as surprise number four.

Ike, feeling satisfied with himself, glanced around. All was quiet in the kitchen. Boy was finally asleep. And so was Cousin Jake, snoring and sputtering once more. From the expression on his face it looked like he was dreaming of the taste of that banana skin he'd eaten. Tonight instead of counting sheep, Ike fell asleep counting the hours till he'd see Papa.

The morning smell of Mama's wonderful coffee roused Ike from the sleep he'd fallen into. He hadn't awakened Mama to stand guard. He stepped over Cousin Jake's now empty perrina and staggered into the kitchen. Sunlight streamed through the white lace curtains and danced on the worn linoleum floor.

"I'm sorry, Jake," Mama was saying. "I have only enough porridge for the *kinder.* We can afford only day-old rolls or bread. But if you dunk it in the coffee, it's not too hard."

Cousin Jake dunked and slurped. Coffee dribbled down his beard.

Boy sat curled in Mama's lap where she spoke to him softly in Yiddish and fed him pieces of her roll dipped in coffee.

Boy slurped and coffee dribbled down his chin just like it dribbled down Cousin Jake's. They were like the amateur boxers Ike went to watch in the basement gym at St. Jerome's Church—each in his corner taking time out but keeping an eye on each other.

Bessie, dressed and ready for school, ate from a bowlful of steaming porridge. Another bowl and spoon were set up for Ike.

"Good morning, Ikey dear," Mama greeted him. "Spoon yourself some cereal and pour me a second cup of coffee, please. I don't want to get up and cause Boy not to digest. And you should have called me to take over so you could have slept more."

Ike didn't answer. He just poured Mama's coffee and reached for the pan she always kept warming on the back burner. Into the coffee cup he spooned some choate, the thick, gooey, evaporated milk Mama loved so much and Ike detested. He even hated the smell of the skin that formed on the top of the cooking milk. He was glad the cut up orange peels Mama always kept on the stove to send up good kitchen smells overpowered the milk odor.

He handed Mama the cup, stopped to pat Boy's furry head, then spooned himself some cereal and sat down. He ate the steaming porridge and glanced at Cousin Jake seated in Papa's kitchen chair. That sight made him more determined than ever. Somehow he would try to get to Papa and make him better, by giving him hope and love. Perhaps it was a silly, impossible dream. But like Mama often said, "You never know until you try. To say

impossible is like giving yourself a reason to do nothing." *On the other hand,* Ike thought, *getting onto the hospital ship probably was impossible.*

But right now, he had to get to school. He finished his cereal in a couple of gulps and let Bessie tell just one more silly riddle about a chicken and an egg.

Then, for the first time, Mama asked what she thought was a riddle. "So tell me, kinder," she said, "who will take care of Boychik while I sell cloth and take Cousin Jake looking for a job? Left here, Boy will chew up the house and everything in it, for sure."

Cousin Jake shuddered at her words and choked on a crumb.

"Give Jake a hit on the back," Mama instructed Ike.

Ike was delighted to do just that.

"Not so hard, Ikey. What's the matter with you?" Mama said. "So now answer already my riddle. You give up? So I'll tell you. You, Ikey, will have to come up with a plan."

5
A NEW BOY
IN THE CLASS

"Just don't leave Boy here to chew up the furniture while Jake and I are away," Mama warned. "That's all I ask."

"Don't worry, Mama. I will think of something," Ike said, putting his cereal bowl in the sink. *And I will think of a way to get to Papa, today!* Ike added to himself. "Maybe Murray the newsman could watch Boy while I'm in school." If Papa was home, Ike thought, he'd let Boy stay with him while he slept days to ready himself for his hard night's work at the pants factory. But Papa wasn't home.

Ike washed and dressed quickly, then he and Bessie left to find Murray the newsman. But today Murray was nowhere in sight and a note was tacked on his newsstand. It was wrinkled and ink-blotched, but two words were clearly written—"gone fishin'!" Ike read the words out loud, understanding Murray's way of saying he'd taken the day off.

It was getting late now and Ike didn't want to get into trouble at school. He'd already been late a couple of times when he had to help Mama carry bundles of cloth to her basement shop. So, rather than being tardy again in order to find someone to watch Boy, Ike decided to be on time, and maybe have one smart puppy, as well.

"Here, Boy," Ike called. Boy came running, slipping and sliding on the linoleum.

Ike bent down. Boy jumped into his arms.

Ike put the tiny puppy inside his jacket

where he hoped Boy would just listen and sleep. So, with Bessie sworn to secrecy but giggling at his side, and Boy, the dog scholar, just a furry lump inside his jacket, Ike set off for Public School 43. Ike was not yet thinking like a man.

Ike and Bessie entered the redbrick school building just as the bell rang.

"Hurry to your class, Bessie," Ike said, giving her a gentle push in the right direction. "The late bell's gonna ring any minute now."

But Bessie insisted on saying goodbye to Boy. And these days, more than ever, once Bessie made up her mind, Ike could spit wooden nickels and it wouldn't change a thing. But with Papa away, Ike felt sorry for Bessie and gave in to her every whim.

"I just want to kiss Boy goodbye and tell him to be good. Like Mama did to me the first day I went to school," Bessie whispered to Ike, pulling at his sleeve. Boy wiggled inside Ike's jacket and licked a warm wet spot right through Ike's shirt. Ike hoped Boy wouldn't wet him in other ways as well.

"Boy is hidden inside my jacket," Ike said. "If you talk to my jacket, it will look funny." Bessie made a sad face with her own special pout. "Oh, all right, talk to Boy and tell him what you want. But be fast," Ike instructed. "Make believe you're crying and I'll make believe I'm hugging you."

Bessie did just what Ike said to do. Only Bessie, the actress, Sarah Heartburn, as Mama called her, didn't just sob . . . she wailed. Before Ike could stifle her with his hand over her mouth, Boy, at the sound of the first sob, pushed his head out of the jacket, his ears flapping as he looked for Bessie. Ike quickly hugged her so no one would hear her words or notice the dog.

"Be a good Boy," was all Bessie could get out before she was quieted by Boy, himself, who licked her on the mouth. "Feh!" she said and raced off to class.

Ike skipped up the stairs to the fifth floor clutching his books and lunch bag with one arm and the right side of his jacket with the other. Huffing and puffing at the fifth floor stair

landing, he found trouble . . . and her name was Miss Ivanovius, his teacher from last year.

He waited for her to open the door to the hall. But she just stood there glaring at him. He hoped Boy wouldn't poke his head out. Finally, she spoke. "Aren't you going to open the door for a lady?" Miss Ivanovius asked. "Where are your manners, Ike Greenberg?"

Ike was frozen. If he stopped clutching his books to his chest, the tiny wriggling puppy would surely pop his head out. And Miss Ivanovius, of all people, would never understand.

"Well? I'm waiting!" She huffed and her eyeglasses fell from her nose and hung on the chain around her thin neck. Then she opened the door herself, turned, pointed a crooked finger at Ike and muttered, "Fix your jacket. It's all lumpy. You disagreeable boy!"

Of course at the mention of his name, Boy couldn't be stopped. He pushed his head out of Ike's jacket and, with that crooked finger waving in front of him, licked his lips. He would have bitten it for sure if Ike hadn't whirled around in the nick of time and pushed Boy back inside.

Just then the late bell rang causing Miss Ivanovius to turn and look upward toward the sound and away from Ike, and to hurry off saying, "Where are my bifocals? Everything looks like a lumpy and wriggling blur without them."

So Ike, breathing a sigh of relief, raced to his nearby classroom and slid into it with the faint echo of the late bell still hanging in the air. With this good excuse of not having time to take off his outer jacket and hang it on his hook in the wardrobe, Ike sat down at his desk.

Throughout opening exercises Boy was as good as Baby Murray after a feeding. Ike was glad to have a seat in the back, where most of the thirty-nine kids in his class couldn't see him. Ike had patted Boy during the pledge of allegiance, and the breathing exercises must have lulled the small puppy to sleep. All went well during arithmetic. During civics, Ike piled his books on his desk to shield the view of the moving lump inside his jacket. When Mrs.

Frye, Ike's eighth grade teacher, told him to put his books away so he could write properly, Ike thought his secret would be discovered and squirmed nervously. But the teacher just went back to correcting the current events test papers.

Mrs. Frye was a small, gray-haired woman who spoke sweetly. "Time for our weekly spelling bee," she said. "Girls line up over here," she added, pointing to the wardrobe side of the room. The girls immediately obeyed, with Sylvia Myerson in the lead. Ike tried to cover Boy's ears with his hands so he wouldn't hear the teacher's next words. But Mrs. Frye, pointing to the window side of the room, did not say, "Boys over here," as she usually did. Ike waited. She cleared her throat and started to speak. Ike was relieved when all she said was, "And the rest of the class line up over here."

Most of the boys were groaning over the thought of a spelling bee and took their time getting up. Ziggie groaned the loudest.

"You can do it," Ike encouraged him. Last spring, Ike had helped him improve his spelling, at least a little bit.

"Come on. Over here, boys." Mrs. Frye's additional announcement, made in a louder voice, caught Ike by surprise.

One Boy obeyed immediately. Only he had flapping ears and a tail. Before Ike could do a thing about it, Boy pushed out of the bottom of his jacket, and wagging his tail, wriggled his way over to exactly where the teacher stood pointing and calling, "No stalling. Come over here right now. BOYS! BOYS! BOYS!" The puppy laid down, putting his legs straight out behind him and resting his chin on the top of one of Mrs. Frye's black shoes.

Squeals of delighted surprise filled the classroom as the children nudged each other and pointed to the puppy. Ike stifled a gasp and just walked calmly to the boy's lineup, acting as surprised as the others at the sight of the dog.

"Now what do we have here?" Mrs. Frye exclaimed.

Then Boy got up and leaned against her long black skirt, leaving brown hairs on it. Ike prayed Mrs. Frye liked dogs. And God must have said yes to his prayers because Mrs. Frye didn't scold Boy or anyone else. Instead, she joked and said, "He thinks he's a new boy in our class."

The children giggled and Boy wagged his tail merrily at the sound of what Mrs. Frye didn't know was his real name.

"Now where did you come from? The street no doubt." She answered her own question and Ike breathed another sigh of relief. "We'd better keep the door closed from now on," Mrs. Frye instructed, adjusting the white paper cuffs pinned on her blouse sleeve to keep the material from getting chalked up.

Ike was glad Mrs. Frye was a dog lover. All would have been well if only she hadn't picked up Boy. For when she did, Boy looked at her, eye to eye, and then quickly licked her right on the lips!

"UGH!" she said, quickly putting Boy down. She sputtered, "Who will volunteer to take this dog away? I can't leave the class alone to take the dog downstairs and outside."

Hands waved and there were calls of, "OO, OO, OO, choose me." But Ike was the first to respond with the words, "I'll help you," and he called, "here Boy, here Boy." Ike had to lean against a nearby wooden desk to catch his balance when Boy leaped into his arms.

"Don't return until you've found a good place for that dog," Mrs. Frye ordered. "Sammy, go with Ike and open the doors for him. Wait, I have a better idea," she added. "Go from room to room and see if you can find the dog's owner," she suggested. "It probably followed some child to school today. Be sure to apologize to the teachers for the interruption." Then, turning to the girl's side of the classroom she said, "Class, the first word in your spelling bee is: disgusting." She said the word as she wiped at her mouth with a handkerchief she'd had tucked in her cuffs. "DIS-GUST-ING!"

Ike, with Boy in his arms and Sammy next to him, couldn't have been happier as they quietly made their way down the hall. Mrs. Frye had just given them the day off because there was no "good" place for "that dog" until five o'clock when Mama would be home again. And Mrs. Frye had just given Ike a good idea. He planned to go to each class that had in it one of the East 136th Street army of boys. They would know it was his dog so they'd catch on for sure when in each class he'd announce, "Mrs. Frye said, 'Anyone who knows whose dog this is should come with me.' "

He might not be able to get *all* the boys out of school for the afternoon. Some teachers wouldn't allow it. But Ike planned to be very convincing. Surely he'd get enough of his friends free to help him, without their getting in trouble at school, because they each had their teacher's permission to leave. And he would explain to each boy that this was an emergency. They had to help Papa—a visit from friends could make Papa feel like "a million bucks."

Now the boys wouldn't have to wait until Sunday for surprise number three—the hospital visit, and number four—the present of hope and love. Like Mama often said, "Don't waste a gift of time. Use it well." Ike would use the time off from school very well. He didn't want to wait any longer to see Papa on the hospital ship. He wanted to try to make him feel strong enough to come to his Bar Mitzvah about a month away. Time was running out.

Mama was right. Ike thought of her words.

"You've got to hope. You've got to believe. Why look for dark clouds when you can still see some blue sky?" Even the doctors didn't know much about TB. Papa had to keep hoping to get better, too, and Ike wanted to make sure he did.

So now Sammy, Ike, and Boy went to each seventh and eighth grade classroom, except Miss Ivanovius's, asking if anyone knew the dog's owner. It was easier than they expected. Most teachers let one boy out of class to help, not knowing there was already an army of helpers waiting in the hall. Sammy, Dave, Bernie, and Sol, Patrick, Danny, Tony, and James all wanted to help Papa in this emergency. But they had some questions.

"Shh . . . I'll explain everything soon," Ike said to them before going into the next classroom. "You gotta be quiet or the plan won't work." Sammy gave Dave one last poke and they all settled down. Only Joey and Herbie couldn't go because they were in the same class with Morton Weinstein and the teacher had selected Morton as the volunteer to help find the dog's owner. Ike was glad that his changing voice had only cracked once during his class announcements, and he only tripped over his own feet twice.

By eleven o'clock, with Boy as their unexpected hero, Ike and Sammy and most of the East 136th Street army of boys were on their way to the hospital ship to find Papa.

"But couldn't we catch something and get sick?" Morton asked as they headed up the block. "Breathe in germs?" No one paid much attention to Morton who often worried about getting sick.

"We'll be in the open air—on a boat," Ike explained. "Or we'll just hold our breath." Ike still was not thinking like a man.

"I can't get directions from my old man," Patrick Murphy said. "He'd direct me right back to school." It was Mr. Murphy's directions the boys had followed last March to get to the filming of *Way Down East*. Patrick's father delivered furniture and knew how to get everywhere.

Ike didn't think Mama would like this plan one bit, either. If she knew about it, she'd forbid him to go. She didn't even like him to play with Morton when he had a cold, so she'd hate the idea of Ike being amongst tuberculosis germs. And skipping school would definitely cause Mama trouble.

Since they couldn't go home for their bikes at this time of the day, they planned to use their milk or lunch money as fare for the train and take the Third Avenue El. What Ike didn't tell his friends was that he wasn't certain how to get to the hospital ship or how to get on board.

Ike was carrying Boy under his arm now like a bundle of cloth. The dog hung limply enjoying the rhythm of Ike's steps. Ike decided he would definitely not take Boy to school again. He hoped Murray the newsman liked puppies as much as he liked "goin' fishin'," because Ike planned to leave Boy with Murray tomorrow. And most of all, he hoped Boy would behave on the train and wouldn't bark or give the boys away when and if they got to the hospital ship at the pier near Bellevue Hospital . . . at least not until the right moment.

6
AT THE HOSPITAL SHIP

As the El train whizzed past brick apartment houses with quilts airing out on fire escapes, Ike put worries of Cousin Jake aside, relaxed, and peered into the windows. He caught glimpses of a fat, hairy-chested man, a woman stirring a pot, a couple hugging, a child being scolded, and some men playing cards at a kitchen table.

The train passed factories where people were busy working at sewing machines or loading boxes. It passed storefronts with colorful signs in the windows. Soon, to the rumble sound was added a clink and clank noise as the train crossed over the 149th Street Bridge. Water shimmered below and the gray metal trellis glistened in the early autumn sunlight.

The twelve boys played with the puppy they'd smuggled aboard the train and laughed about Boy getting them out of school. Eagerly they rode toward the Manhattan piers—to the floating hospital ship. At one station stop Ike read a poster that warned: MISTER. IF YOU CAN'T DO THE TIME . . . BETTER NOT DO THE CRIME, and he clutched Boy tightly, wondering if he was caught with Boy would he have to do time in jail. Twice Boy almost wriggled right out of his lap. None of the passengers seemed to mind that there was a dog on the train. Ike just hoped a conductor wouldn't come aboard this car. Dogs were definitely not allowed.

Ike squirmed and the straw from the seat poked as usual. Tony Golida nudged him and signaled with his eyes for Ike to look at a bearded man wearing a yarmulke, a small circle of cloth covering his head to show reverence to God's glory around and above him. The man was sitting across from the boys and was reading a newspaper, turning pages from back to front.

"What kind of paper is that?" Tony asked. "What are those lines and squiggles instead of ABCs?"

"He's reading *The Forward*, a Yiddish newspaper," Ike explained.

"So, how come it's called *The Forward*, and he's reading it backward?" Tony asked.

"Because it's Hebrew and you read from right to left," Ike answered, getting a warm feeling in his chest. For the man reading *The Forward* made Ike think of Papa, and he knew soon he'd see Papa—maybe even be able to hug him.

The boys bumped and swayed to the train's rhythm. They leaned to one side as the brakes squealed and the train slowed to a halt. But this was not their station.

"Hey, Ikey," Danny asked as the train started up again. "How we gonna get on the hospital ship once we find the pier?"

"We just walk on like we know where we're going," Ike said. "We wave at someone and walk on board. We might even see where the captain steers." He built up the boys' excitement and his own.

"We should've borrowed my uncle's white uniform," James said. "He's a cook. Then we could've dressed Danny up in it, made a red cross out of paper, and pinned it on his pocket. He's so tall he looks old enough to pass for a doctor."

"I can't wait to see the pretty nurses," Sammy said, and made a kissing noise. "Maybe I could bump into one of them and cause a real commotion."

"The bumping idea sounds good," Ike agreed, "but not the commotion."

Dave, not wanting to miss anything, was dashing from one side of the train to the other, so he could look out both door windows and see all the sights almost at once.

Ike took a deep breath. The train smelled like damp dust.

Finally the El train squealed to a halt at the 28th Street stop and the boys quickly got off, hiding Boy in Ike's jacket. Then the East 136th Street army of boys jogged down several blocks to the East River piers, feeling the breeze getting stronger as they neared the water. Boy was allowed to trot along with them. He stopped first to sniff a fire hydrant, then a piece of coal which blackened the furry white spot near his snout.

Ike's heartbeat quickened at the thought of Papa's nearness as they passed Bellevue Hospital and crossed the street to the piers. But his heart almost stood still when he saw the empty pier instead of the hospital ship.

"So where's the boat, Ike?" Morton asked.

"Is this one of your wild goose chases?" Danny said.

Why hadn't he thought to find out the boat schedule—when it left for its ride around Manhattan Island and when it would return. It must be after noon, Ike figured, wondering where the ship would be now. The pier was empty except for a couple of nurses on their lunch break, getting some fresh air and sunshine. They were sitting at the edge of the pier, their white-stockinged legs hanging over the edge.

Boy saw them first, raced over to them, barked and snatched a piece of bologna right out of the sandwich one of the nurses was holding.

"Hey, come back here, you little rascal!" she shouted, and started to chase after the puppy.

Ike chased after him, too, and grabbed him just as the last of the bologna disappeared. Boy licked his lips enjoying the taste.

"I'm sorry." Ike tipped his cap politely and apologized to the nurse who stood by his side. She was short, he noticed. He felt tall and big next to her. Then remembering the small bag with the salami sandwich he had tucked inside his big jacket pocket, he took it out and offered it to the nurse. Ike thought she was the prettiest woman he had ever seen. Her hair was

dark and bobbed, and she wore lip coloring and rouge. "My dog stole your lunch so please have mine instead," he said.

"Oh, I couldn't," she said shyly. "What would you eat?"

"Never mind about me," Ike said, "you'll be hungry and you probably have a lot of sick people to take care of yet today." Ike tried to push the lunch bag into her hands, but she pushed it back.

The boys sauntered over to where Ike and the nurse stood talking and patting the puppy who was in Ike's arms. They stood around. Morton switched weight from one foot to the other. James cleared his throat to push away sudden shyness. Patrick poked Bernie and Sol making them move so he could get a better view of the nurses.

"I wish I'd have spoken to her first," Sammy whispered to Dave.

"She's like a movie star," Dave whispered back, and winked at the nurses.

Some of the boys who'd thought to take their lunch bags unwrapped their sandwiches.

"Those of us who keep kosher will share our lunches, how's that?" Ike suggested, taking his sandwich from the bag. "Then none of us will be hungry."

Before the two nurses knew what was happening, they were surrounded by twelve boys and a wiggly puppy.

"All right," the pretty nurse said, "I'll eat half of your sandwich and you eat the other half."

"Good," Ike said, handing her half of his sandwich. Sharing a sandwich felt almost like a kiss.

"Hey, Ikey," Sammy said, "does sharing sandwiches with nurses count as a mitzvah? Can we tell the rabbi?"

Dave and Morton laughed. Ike didn't. He was trying to act like a gentleman, and he was struggling to keep his voice deep-sounding like a gentleman and not croaking and changing like a thirteen-year-old boy. Besides—Sammy was already a Bar Mitzvah. He should know a mitzvah is a commandment, not just a good deed. Although, it is a good deed as well.

As the group munched the food, they started to talk. "Do you know what time the Floating Hospital ship of St. John's Guild returns?" Ike asked.

"Not till four o'clock, unless it gets chilly," the pretty nurse said.

"This time of year it sometimes comes in early if the wind shifts," the blond nurse added. "The ship's doctors and nurses don't take a chance on the patients getting chilled even though they're wrapped in blankets."

Ike looked at the sky. The sun was shining brightly and he could feel the warmth through his jacket. He could hear the water slapping against the wooden pier. He searched above for a dark cloud but there was none.

"Why are you here?" the very pretty nurse asked.

"Well, you see, I've been sent by the fire department," Ike quickly replied. The other boys stared at Ike not knowing what he was talking about.

"The fire department?" The nurse looked puzzled.

Ike started to make up a crazy story about being a special hospital boat checker sent by the city to see that there were no violations. He'd heard that word "violations" from the fire chief when he talked to the kids at the assembly in school. Swirling in Ike's mind were crazy plans of charging on board the ship and finding Papa. Only hours before, Ike had pulled off a wild scheme to get his friends out of school—so why not another one now? But as he looked out at the river, he could almost feel Papa getting nearer.

Suddenly Ike couldn't go on with his story. He found himself stopping and wanting to think things out more. In just one month he'd be thirteen. He would celebrate his Bar Mitzvah. He'd be considered a man. He'd be responsible for his own actions. He'd better start thinking about the words that usually just flew out of his mouth.

"Forget what I just said," Ike told the nurse and went on. "What I meant was that my papa is on the hospital ship."

To his surprise, and to his friends' surprise

as well, Ike found himself talking on and on, telling the truth. He told the nurse about studying for his Bar Mitzvah and about his need to see Papa. He told how Papa has TB and has been away from home so long.

It seemed like a miracle to him that he was actually feeling more and more like a man— maybe even starting to think like a man. Ike liked the way this nurse was listening to his every word, stopping only to feed Boy the end of a hard roll. Boy just held the chunk in his mouth or dropped it and, as Ike set him down on the wooden pier, Boy moved it around with his paws, the way a kitten plays with a ball of yarn.

Ike also liked the feeling of being honest with this young woman who had brown eyes that looked like windows to her heart. Ike pointed to the other boys and continued.

"So my friends and I came all the way from the Bronx on the Third Avenue El. We raced from Third Avenue here to see the hospital ship." Ike blushed as his voice cracked and changed octaves, but went on. "And now—"

"Wait," the nurse interrupted. She kicked a pebble through the space between the boards of the pier and Ike heard it splash in the water below. The nurse was tilting her head suspiciously at Ike. "You don't live around East 136th Street, do you?"

"Sure," Morton said. "We're the East 136th Street army!"

But the nurse was looking at Ike. "Is your name, by any chance . . . Ike?"

"Yes," Ike said, puzzled. "But how did you guess that?"

The nurse started to smile then went on. "Is your papa a tall man named Harry Greenberg?" Ike nodded his head, answering yes, and was really surprised when she added, "So you're the Ikey Mr. Greenberg talks about so much. I feel as if I know you. Your papa is a wonderful man. He's been very sick, poor man. When he comes back from his day trips on the hospital ship, I've been one of the nurses that takes care of him at Bellevue Hospital across the street. When he talks about you his eyes light up with pride and I think it makes him feel better. So I often talk to him about you."

Ike kind of puffed up his chest feeling proud hearing the nurse's words about Papa.

"I heard how you were an extra in the movies last summer," the nurse added.

"We were in it too," Morton Weinstein said.

"Me too," Sammy said.

"I've met your nice mama. I heard also how you take good care of your little sister. Bessie is her name, right?"

"Hey, she knows all about you, Ikey," James Higgins added.

"But what makes your papa so sad is that he is not home to help you study for your Bar Mitzvah. He wanted so much to do that."

Ike cleared his throat, ready to ask the important question. By now, Ike had read the lettered pin the very pretty nurse wore on her uniform, and knew her name was Shirley. Now was the time to hear how it sounded. "Shirley," he said slowly, as if trying the sounds on for size, "do you think we could visit my papa on the hospital ship? Maybe he could hear me recite one of my blessings and we'd both feel better. We're here to bring him hope, a mitzvah, to help him get better."

"I'm afraid you need a doctor's permission to board the ship. The doctors don't like children to come too close to patients with tuberculosis. You have to be an adult."

Ike wished the pretty nurse hadn't called him a child.

"You can't fight City Hall," the blond nurse said.

"But, Ike, you know I think you're right. Your papa was beginning to feel better, then he started worrying about this and that, his family, and your Bar Mitzvah. And he seemed to get weaker and quieter. I think seeing you would help." .

As they thought, they all watched Boy playing with the end of the hard roll the nurse had given him. He licked it, growled at it, and pushed it closer and closer to the edge of the pier. He picked it up in his mouth and shook it. He was having a wonderful time.

"What if . . ." Ike started to say.

"I know," Shirley interrupted. "What if you come back here around four o'clock."

Ike was amazed as she finished his very thought.

"I'll be back then to help wheel the patients across the street to Bellevue Hospital," Shirley added. "It's a free country. You're allowed on the pier."

"And would you wheel Papa where I could see him and maybe speak to him?" Ike asked.

"I'll make sure to wheel your papa off the ship, then slowly down the pier. You can wave to him, and without coming too close, surprise him and recite the blessing he wants so much to hear."

Ike smiled a smile bigger than he'd ever smiled before. Boy was leaning over the pier. He held the hard roll in his mouth and stared down at his reflection in the water. It reminded Ike of something Papa once told him when Ike was being greedy.

"Don't be like the dog who, with a bone in its mouth, looks at its reflection in a brook and seeing a bigger bone drops his to go after it."

Ike grabbed Boy away from the edge before he fell in. He told Shirley, "Seeing Papa on the pier will be enough for me." Seeing the inside of the boat could wait for another time.

Shirley gently hugged Ike good-bye and the nurses went back to work walking across the street to the big hospital nearby. Ike enjoyed the feeling of her hug and the scent of her rouge and powder long after she was out of sight. Boy growled jealously and Sammy wolf-whistled. Dave, Patrick, Danny, and Sol followed Sammy's lead. Each tried to wolf-whistle the loudest.

The boys sunbathed awhile, collected some flat stones and sent them skimming across the water, then walked up to watch the automobiles on First Avenue. They wanted to see who would be the first to spot those quiet electric trucks, like the ones from R. H. Macy and Co., or how many flivvers, their word for Fords, they'd see. They looked for taxis—Yellows and Checkers. But best of all, they tried to spot Luxor cabs, which were all white and had flat chrome pipes that snaked in and out of the motor hood. It was said that when you sighted a Luxor cab, if you spit into your palm and then punched the blob with your fist before the taxi reached the corner, you were guaranteed twenty-four hours of good luck.

It wasn't until three-thirty that Ike spotted the Luxor cab, did the required spitting, and punched the blob before the taxi reached the corner. So at four o'clock when the army of boys, worrying about how late it was getting, returned to the pier, Ike felt excited and Luxor-cab lucky as he waited to surprise Papa. The boys looked up and down the river expectantly, each wanting to be the first to spot the ship. Finally they heard a distant horn blast and Ike, Sammy, and Dave yelled, "Here it comes." The boys watched as the big white hospital ship, with its red trim, was guided to the pier by the Moran tugboat. The single smokestack, round-bellied tug nudged the ship carefully to its berth.

Ike could see blanket-wrapped patients,

some in deck chairs, others on stretchers or in wheelchairs. The ship's nurses and volunteers waved to the Bellevue Hospital nurses waiting to help them return the patients needing hospital care. Just as the tugboat tooted its horn announcing the arrival, Shirley waved to the boys from the end of the pier where she stood. Ike's heart beat loudly as he raced toward her. Boy barked and nipped at his heels as he ran with Ike. Sammy huffed and puffed but kept up with the army of boys following Ike's lead. Just as Ike got to Shirley he tripped over his own big feet and she practically had to catch him. Ike leaned over and picked up Boy so no one would see his red face.

Then as the ship clanked into the dock, he could feel inside the joy and surprise he knew Papa would soon feel. He hugged Boy till he squealed. Just as Shirley started up the gangplank, Ike said, "Don't tell Papa we're here—we want to surprise him." She waved and nodded in agreement.

Soon patients on stretchers or in wheelchairs were being wheeled off the ship, and others able to walk were aided by nurses and volunteers. One man in a wheelchair strummed a ukelele but some other patients looked too pale and sick to even smile.

Soon, in this parade of blanket wrapped patients, Ike saw Shirley pushing a wheelchair with Papa in it. Tall Papa seated was the same height as the small nurse, Shirley, who pushed him. When he got closer, Ike felt tears come to his eyes and a lump grow in his throat. He wanted to run over and throw his arms around Papa—to make Papa notice him. He wanted to bury his head in Papa's chest and be a little boy again. But he knew he'd promised not to go too close. So he hugged Boy tighter and then, after Ike made sure his cap was covering his head securely, he just started chanting really loud the beginning of the Torah blessing, which the rabbi had said must be recited before reading.

"BO-RE-CHU ES A-DO-NOI HA-ME-VO-RACH! BO-RUCH A-DO-NOI HA-ME-VO-RACH LE-O-LOM VO-ED! . . . Praise the Lord, to whom our praise is due! Praised be the Lord, to whom our praise is due, now and for ever! . . ." Ike translated the Hebrew words beginning the blessing. He didn't think his voice could be this loud.

Papa looked so sad slumped down in the wheelchair, but by the word *LE-O-LOM* Papa grew tall in his chair and was looking around. Shirley was pointing in Ike's direction. Other men and women in wheelchairs turned their heads toward the sound of the chanting. Ike was waving, as he shouted, "You will get well soon, Papa!"

The other boys were waving and shouting. "Get well soon, Mr. Greenberg," Morton Weinstein yelled.

"We miss you," James Higgins added. And Boy was yelping.

"Ikey!" Papa said, smiling now, after Ike had finished the blessing. Ike could feel Papa's surprise mixing with his own joy at having given it. But he had to strain to hear Papa's weak voice. "That was good. But puvulya— relax, slow down—you don't have to pray like you are about to miss a train. What's that you are holding? It's not a rat, is it?"

"No, Papa. It's my puppy, Boy." Ike

stroked the white furry spot on Boy's head.

Then Papa waved weakly and did something Ike had never seen him do before. He put his hand to his lips and threw Ike a kiss, and Ike was sure he heard the words, "I love you."

"I love you too, Papa, and you will get well and be at my Bar Mitzvah. You'll see." Even though Ike was about twenty feet away, he was sure Papa wiped tears away, and then looked up at the sky.

"We'll see," was the last Ike heard Papa say that day, as Shirley started to wheel him off down the pier and across the street to Bellevue Hospital.

"I'll be here to get your papa off this ship on any sunny Tuesday or Thursday at four o'clock," Shirley called to Ike. "The hospital ship only runs for a few more weeks in the fall."

"I'll be back on Tuesday!" Ike shouted to Papa and Shirley. "Thanks," he added. Then the boys hurried to catch the train before the rush hour crush of people would pack them like a closed up accordian.

The boys were all joking and happy about

their lunch with the nurses. "I could've watched those nurses wiggly-walk all the way across the street to the hospital," Danny said, and Sammy wolf-whistled. "Only we'd have been late and missed the train," Danny added.

James Higgins teased, saying, "Danny Mantussi is so tall he doesn't have to worry about being late. If he falls over he's halfway home."

Ike only half heard the joking. His thoughts were still on Papa. Ike felt as if God himself had patted him on the shoulder. He knew he'd done a mitzvah for sure.

He would work hard and practice hard and maybe Papa really would get well enough to be at the Bar Mitzvah. That would be the best surprise ever.

7
HOPING, DREAMING, AND WORRYING

The boys were happy as they rode home from the hospital ship, bumping along on the train. Each boy was convincing the other how much better Ike's papa looked after seeing all of them. "I think some color went back in his cheeks," Morton said.

"His eyes got a bit brighter," Sammy added.

"We were too far to tell," Dave reminded them.

Boy poked his head out of Ike's jacket and squeaked a yawn.

Ike thought Papa perked up after the visit. But even perked up, Papa still looked pretty sick slumped over in the wheelchair. That's why Ike hadn't mentioned Cousin Jake to his papa. Papa might feel Cousin Jake was taking over: sitting in his chair, listening to Ike chant his prayers, and eating Mama's good cooking. Doing the things Papa loved to do.

Back at the apartment, Ike, carrying Boy, opened the door. Both of them sniffed a wonderful aroma and headed toward it. Mama was busy in the kitchen, at the stove, rendering chicken fat and frying up onions in it till they were crisp. Grivenas it was called. You could almost see it in the curls of steam in the air, and Ike's mouth watered anticipating the tasty, crunchy morsels Mama would spoon inside day-old bread.

Ike was always proud of the way Mama could make a delicious meal even when there seemed to be almost no food left.

"Ikey," Mama said without looking up, "where have you been? You and Boy? It's dinner time already."

Ike was in no hurry to tell that he'd left school early, or that he'd taken Boy to school, or that without permission he had visited Papa. Mama would be upset for sure, and Ike was in no hurry for trouble. As Mama would say, "Everything in its time." And now was not the right time to explain. Ike could see Mama was too busy turning the frying onions with a fork so they wouldn't burn, and moving back quickly when the fat spattered. Ike decided she was much too busy to listen to the long story of his day.

"Later, Mama," Ike said. "I will explain later. I don't want you to listen now and burn yourself at the stove."

"So then, go wash up, Ike, and tell Bessie and Cousin Jake to get ready for dinner. You and I will talk later."

Later was better than now, Ike felt, relieved to postpone a worrisome moment.

Cousin Jake was in the parlor sleeping in Papa's chair waiting to be called in to dinner as if he was a king, Ike thought. When Ike put Boy down, the puppy raced right over to Jake and pulled on his trouser cuff. Cousin Jake awoke with a shudder. Then the furry whirlwind started twirling around in circles chasing his own tail and growling till Bessie clapped her hands. "Boy, come here," she called, sitting down on the parlor floor and spinning around, imitating the puppy. If Boy had been a child, Ike thought, the dog would have laughed out loud at the gleeful, dizzy feeling the spinning produced. Then as Boy and Bessie collapsed on the floor, Boy wiggled closer to Bessie's face and licked her on the lips.

Cousin Jake sounded like Mama. "Feh!" he said. Ike had no trouble understanding this Yiddish sound of disgust.

"Come everyone for a something to eat," Mama called.

"Helloi." Jake greeted Ike with a smile. Ike ignored him. Bessie ran over and even climbed up onto Jake's lap. She pulled his whiskers as if he'd always lived in the house with her.

Ike could feel his muscles tighten. "Bessie, get off there and go wash your hands," he grumbled at his sister, the traitor. To Jake, all he said was, "Mama said get ready."

At the table Mama was far too busy talking about her day with Jake, searching for a job. Ike was glad this too was not the right time to tell about his own day. He wanted to tell Mama about it when no one else was around to add to the trouble.

"First we went to the pants factory," Mama said. "No work. Then we went to the shirt factory and the tie factory. No work. Then we stopped by the butcher . . . no work." Mama went on, "But he did give me a package of lung and miltz for Boy and even threw in a calf's foot."

Mama lifted Boy up and held him out in front of her. She looked into his eyes and he looked into hers. She spoke to Boy as if he understood each word.

"So, Boychik, now is your turn to learn to share. In your bowl is the lung and miltz, so enjoy, but the calf's foot, maybe you will share with the rest of us? I will make from it and the eggs I got, tomorrow's dinner, petcha—and you will have some, too." Boy's tongue seemed to grow to reach her for a lick but Mama held him out too far.

"Petcha! Oh boy!" Bessie said, already tasting the meaty gelatin dish Mama would make, one of her favorites. Boy turned and licked Bessie. "See, he said yes," Bessie said.

Mama set Boy down to eat at his bowl and then served the bread and grivenas to Bessie and Ike, laughing. "See how it all works out? Boy is not only an extra mouth to feed, but a provider of food for the rest of us, also. And I will even be able to bring some petcha to Papa when I visit him on Sunday."

Ike swallowed hard at the mention of Mama's regular Sunday visits to Papa, knowing the doctor had forbidden him to go along. Knowing he had to tell Mama he'd disobeyed.

All Mama and Jake had for dinner was a cup each of sour milk. Mama had prepared it yesterday, smearing sour cream on the rims of two glasses, then pouring milk into them and leaving the milk to culture and become like junket. And even that small portion Mama shared with Bessie. Jake offered to share his with Ike, but Ike refused.

After dinner Mama told Bessie to take Boy with her and go into the other room and play. Then Mama once again insisted that Ike practice his prayers and Torah reading with Cousin Jake. Bessie groaned, not happy to be shooed away. "Everything is Ike, Ike, Ike," she pouted, but obeyed Mama and left the room. Only a few moments later, she came back into the kitchen with a red crayon. She walked quietly to the hanging 1921 wall calendar—the calendar the Democratic Club had given out—the very one on which Ike had been carefully marking off with a red x each day that brought him closer to his Bar Mitzvah; closer to becoming a man.

Quick as a cat pouncing on a mouse, Bessie reached out and made red x marks on the last day of September and all the days of October. When she lifted the page to November, Ike caught her in action.

"Stop that," he said, reaching out to grab her. But Mama quieted him with a look and took Bessie onto her lap.

"Oy, Bessie darling," she soothed. "You are very angry, nu? But you mustn't mark up what isn't yours to mark. When you have your birthday I will make for you a party, you will see. Come in the bedroom with me now and we will talk."

Ike, too, was angry and thought Mama should have given Bessie a slap on the hand. Then he remembered he might have Mama trouble of his own when she found out he'd visited Papa. He hoped she'd be as understanding with him. But it wasn't likely. Jake nudged Ike to get on with the chanting. And as Ike recited the blessing before the Torah, he spoke loudly using up some of his anger at Bessie and also pretending he was on the pier with Papa.

"Good boy!" Cousin Jake praised and smiled till he realized Boy might think he'd called him. But the puppy was asleep in his box, kicking his legs as if dreaming he was racing down the streets with Ike and his friends.

Tonight as Ike read his Torah portion which was about Noah and the Ark he thought about another ship of hope—the hospital ship, and of his visit to it.

"Good that I hear you now—so loud—but bad bad you do no good—mix-up." Cousin Jake interrupted and poked a finger into Ike's shoulder and recited the words without even glancing at the book the way Papa had always done. Ike felt angry and pushed the book away. "You don't want learn." Jake shrugged his shoulders and left the room. He called after him, "You study, study. I be back to hear."

The hours of the evening went by as fast as the day had passed. Soon it was Bessie's bedtime and a little later, after making Ike recite again, Jake said good night.

But Mama and Ike stayed up later than the others. Both had things they needed to talk over. Mama made tea, pouring it into a glass and sipping it through a piece of sugar she put between her teeth. She let Ike suck on the other half of the chunk of sugar she'd chipped from a cone. "Maybe it will make you act a little sweeter to Cousin Jake," she said. They sat at the kitchen table where most important discussions took place. "Jake is a nice man, Ike, a smart man. In Russia, people came from the next little town even to have Jake answer their questions and teach them Torah. They would bring him presents of food and clothing. He will be good to study with. You must give him a chance."

"While I'm giving him a chance," Ike repeated Mama's suggestion but added his own finish, "he might set the whole place on fire with his cigarettes. Cousin Jake is the problem, Mama, not me."

Mama rubbed her fingers against her chin as if that would help her think of a solution.

Ike wanted to be the problem solver himself. Maybe that would be thinking like a man —not needing help from anyone else. So he got up and tiptoed into the dark parlor where Jake was asleep on the cot. He reached down beside Jake to remove the pack of cigarettes that lay at his side but Ike's long legs got tangled in the edge of the quilt. He landed next to Jake. Ike was sure Jake would wake up and be angry, but

Jake just reached over, patted Ike's head, and went back to sleep.

Ike wriggled out of Jake's way and returned to the kitchen to hand Mama the cigarettes. "Good," she said. "I will throw these out and he has no money to buy more. The problem with Jake is solved."

Only Jake's smoking problem was solved, Ike thought. To him Jake was still a big problem just because he was there and Papa wasn't. And how could Jake be so smart if he didn't know not to smoke in bed? Papa was smart . . . not Jake.

Ike did not want to talk about Jake. He wanted to talk about Papa. Now he was ready to tell Mama, everything.

Mama sighed. "Oy, Ikey," she said, "such hard times it is without Papa. And now with your Bar Mitzvah. Now what? I wish, I dream, I could make for you a Bar Mitzvah with a celebration afterward fit for a king—a herring party with boiled potatoes and sliced onions and green peppers and fresh corn bread, cake and wine. But this I can't promise you."

Ike thought Mama must be hungry the way she was talking about all this food.

"Don't worry, Mama. That's not what I care about."

"So tell me, Ikey, what would make this Bar Mitzvah special for you? In just a few weeks it will be November third, the big day."

"What would make my Bar Mitzvah special to me is something I can't have." Ike could hardly get the words out. He didn't want to upset Mama but he didn't want to hide the truth, either. Not now when he was starting to think like a man. He would ease into telling her, he decided. Mama reached across the table and put her two hands over his.

"Tell me, Ikey, dear," she urged.

"What I want most is for Papa to be with me, not just to hear me but to be there to have an aliyah, to bless me . . . and maybe if you could make your special yeast cake. That would be a Bar Mitzvah to remember."

Mama smiled and patted Ike's curly hair. Then she clicked her tongue. "You never know," she said. "Like Papa says, puvulya—relax and it will all work out."

"I don't think so this time, Mama," Ike said. "I saw Papa today."

"You what?" Mama's blue eyes opened wide and she almost dropped the glass of tea she'd just taken to her lips. "Where?"

"I went to the hospital ship and I waited and saw him when he got off. I even chanted my blessing for him." Ike explained, "I didn't sneak on the ship, though."

"You didn't go close to him, did you?" Mama's eyes filled with a look of terror. "The doctors said to me that TB is catching."

"No, Mama." Ike tried to calm her. As he feared, she was very upset, and he felt sorry. He patted her shoulder and went on explaining. "This nurse, Shirley, told me where to stand. She said it would be good for him if I talked, and safe for me as long as it was from a distance. She said she thought that my talking to him would help even more than fresh sea air, and that doctors don't know everything, especially about TB."

"Shirley," Mama said. "Papa's nurse Shirley you spoke to? I know now who you mean. What a *shana maidele*, such a pretty girl, and so kind to Papa. Such a good nurse." Mama took a deep breath and let it out slowly. Then she spoke again. "She is smart that Shirley."

Ike could see Shirley in his mind and even hear her voice. She was pretty all right. Even her voice was pretty.

"I count the minutes until Sunday when I visit Papa again," Mama said. "How slowly the time passes. How was he? Tell me every word he said—every look. Ikey, tell already." Mama was practically looming over him with anticipation.

So Ike repeated the day's happenings as if he were a newsreel shown before the main feature at the movies, and Mama's eyes clouded over. But he ended with, "I don't know if this time, Mama, even with a chance of seven surprises, everything will all work out, if Papa will be well enough to come to my Bar Mitzvah. He looked so tired . . . so pale."

"Everything in time," Mama said as if comforting herself. "Everything in time." But time was moving on. In a little more than four weeks Ike would have his Bar Mitzvah.

"But sometimes you have to help things to

work out," Ike said, "and that's what I'm going to try to do. Papa looked better after my visit. It really was like the rabbi says—the mitzvah of Bikkur Cholim—the giving of hope and cheer to the sick. And Shirley said I could visit Papa on Tuesdays and Thursdays at four o'clock. From a distance is better than nothing and at least I can practice with him." Ike looked directly into Mama's eyes. "You're not angry?"

"Who could be angry at a son who longs to help his Papa? Who? Good luck, Ikey. Who's to know what's right or wrong with TB? Just don't go near enough for him to breathe on you. You mustn't get sick yourself. That's important! And as for the yeast cake. That I can promise you. I will start saving the butter and flour and sugar and yeast and we will see what we will see. So now go to sleep my Bar Mitzvah boy." Mama kissed his forehead savoring the feeling of Ike's closeness as if it was a treat that soon might be a rare delicacy.

"Are you going to sleep now?" Ike asked.

"No. I must cook the petcha and put it in the ice box overnight to gel. Tomorrow will be another busy day of looking for work for Jake."

"Then I'll help you," Ike said, and rolled up the sleeves on his shirt.

So together Ike and Mama cooked the calf's foot in a pot of water to make soup stock. And as they peeled and chopped onions, their eyes burned and teared more than usual as they shed some tears for Papa as well. Then Mama added the vegetables to the soup stock, took the meat off the bone, and cut it up. She added salt and pepper and fresh garlic. Ike prepared the hard-boiled egg, mashing the yolk with the light-colored, souplike liquid and slicing in the egg white. Mama poured the petcha into a crockery bowl and placed it in the ice box to gel overnight.

Then Mama washed the pot and Ike dried it. After Mama wiped off the salt and pepper shaker and hung the dish towel on the hook over the sink, she and Ike smiled at each other with satisfaction.

"So maybe like the gelatin, in the morning everything will come together and be clear and delicious." Mama was able to give Ike a flicker of hope. Then she and Ike looked in on Bessie. Mama kissed her own finger then touched it to Bessie's forehead to kiss her without waking her up. Ike did the same. When Bessie was asleep the sight of her filled Ike's heart with love. It was when she was awake that was the problem. Mama and Ike hugged and said good night. They settled down in their rooms.

In a while Ike heard Mama's distant snore. But for Ike sleep didn't seem strong enough to push past his worries about Papa and the Bar Mitzvah. And he surely couldn't take Boy to school again tomorrow.

8
GET READY, GET SET, GO . . .

Murray the newsman loved Boy. They growled at each other, played tug-of-war with a rolled up *Bronx Home News,* and even shared a roll and butter. Ike and Bessie went off to school each day certain that Boy was in good hands. Ike eagerly looked forward to the Tuesday and Thursday afternoons on which he visited Papa.

At four o'clock on Tuesday, a sunny but cool mid-October day, Ike waited with Shirley on the pier. They sat side by side on a three-beamed wooden pile banded together with a giant metal rope. At the blast of the tugboat's horn, they got up and stood next to each other. This time when Papa, wrapped in a green woolen blanket and propped up in a wheelchair, was wheeled off the ramp by one of the ship's nurses, he looked this way and that till he found Ike and waved to him. But it was a very weak wave. To Ike, Papa looked even paler than on last Thursday.

"He had a bad night," Shirley said, and she started to walk to where Papa waited. "But he seems a bit better just from seeing you," she called to Ike over her shoulder.

Ike chanted the blessing almost perfectly and was able to get halfway through the Torah reading before Shirley said time was up. "We don't want your papa to get a chill."

"That was better than last time, Ike," Papa called weakly. "Now you must do something for me."

"Anything you say, Papa," Ike shouted.

"On Sunday Mama told me all about Jake and how you don't like him. Let me tell you something about Jake. There's not a bad bone in his body. Something else even Mama doesn't know." Papa stopped to cough into a handkerchief. He gasped a breath of air and went on. "If it weren't for Jake we wouldn't be in America today. He gave up his place, his money—his ticket—so your mama could come with me to America." Ike strained to hear Papa's fading voice. "Jake never wanted Mama to know because she wouldn't have taken the ticket if she knew it meant keeping Jake back in Russia. She would feel guilty even today. I can't talk more now," Papa said, starting to cough again. "You must practice more with Cousin Jake. You must be nice to him." Papa half-gasped as Shirley wheeled his chair by, clacking over the wooden boards of the pier.

"I love you, Papa. I'll do what you say," Ike called, and waved till Papa was out of sight. All the way home on the train, Ike thought of Papa's words about Cousin Jake.

That night Ike said "Hello" to Cousin Jake before Jake said his usual "Helloi." And at dinner, he didn't look away from Jake. So that was being nice the way Papa asked, Ike thought, but he still didn't like Jake.

"Who wants some more kasha?" Mama offered the big bowl around, saying, "Eat. It's cheap and will fill your belly and keep you healthy." Jake enjoyed another helping of the roasted buckwheat kernels.

After learning from Papa the good things about his cousin, Ike tried to listen to Jake's complaints of no work here—no work there. As the days passed, Ike noticed that Jake looked more and more discouraged. But he just couldn't make himself say something to make Jake feel better.

When Ike practiced his chanting with Jake at night, he even heard the pure tones of Jake's powerful voice as he demonstrated the proper chant for Ike's Torah portion. Before going to sleep Ike prayed not only for Papa's health but for Jake as well—that he might find work soon.

On Thursday, near the end of October, it rained and Ike felt miserable. He wouldn't see Papa or Shirley. The patients couldn't go sailing in bad weather.

At cheder that day, the rabbi spoke again of mitzvahs. He said the reward for doing a mitzvah is doing another mitzvah—that a good deed was a reward in itself. Ike couldn't have agreed more. The rabbi finished the Hebrew school class by reminding the boys to prepare well and practice their Bar Mitzvah speeches.

Ike knew exactly what he wanted to say in his speech, only the words kept getting stuck in his throat. He practiced all weekend, but whenever he thought of how his papa wouldn't be at the shul to come up to chant the blessings for the Torah reading—to have an aliyah—and to hear him chant his Torah portion, he'd get a scooped-out feeling in his stomach and a tight feeling in his throat.

And now today was Halloween—a day when boys and girls wore their jackets inside out because kids shouting "Halloween!" would run up and mark others' clothes with a whack of a sack filled with flour or chalk. The tough guys would fill up stockings with cinders and smack at passersby. It was not a day that Ike celebrated or looked forward to. But the evening of this Halloween Monday turned out to be different.

Jake came home smiling and whistling.

"A work I have now," he said after dinner, and he got up to leave. "I work night. I sleep day. I not bother nobody," he said. "In da morning I have someting for all of you."

And he did. When Ike came in for breakfast Tuesday morning, he blinked with surprise. Then Bessie squealed with delight. There sat Jake, with smudges of flour still on his forehead and cheek, and a big smile on his face. On the table was a heavy, big, black bread. "Fresh pumpernickel for breakfast and fresh hard rolls for Mama. And a sugar cookie for Bessie," Jake said proudly handing one to her. "And a sugar cookie for Ikey," he repeated, handing one to him. "And even a sugar cookie for . . ." he paused and looked around the room.

135

He cleared his throat, leaned back in his chair, put his hand out, and extended his fingers, before finishing the words, "for Boychik."

Boy leaped in the air and snatched the cookie in his mouth. Then he ate it and sneezed. Next he sidled up to Cousin Jake and lay down on his shoe. At first Jake sat stiffly and motionless in his chair. Slowly he relaxed, then went on excitedly.

"I am Cousin Jake . . . The Baker, now!" Cousin Jake, no longer the greena couzina, announced: "I have work in a bakery on Brook Avenue. Now every morning I bring food for 'my family,' " he said, and Ike thought Cousin Jake's eyes got a little cloudy as he pointed to Mama, Ike, Bessie, and Boy. "And, Ike, bring for your papa this sweet roll. It is one like he enjoyed in Russia."

"Thank you," Ike said to Cousin Jake and meant it.

It was a wonderful breakfast with that surprise number five, Cousin Jake's job as a baker, providing good smells and tastes and stomachs filled with rolls and cookies.

Ike waited until Mama left the room before he took out half of the sugar cookie that he'd saved. He handed it to Cousin Jake explaining, "I want to share something with you to thank you for giving up your passage ticket to America so Mama could go first. Papa told me. Mama still doesn't know."

Cousin Jake put his finger to his mouth— the sign in many languages for "keep it quiet." He gestured with a shake of his head and a raise of his shoulders. "Family is for dat," he said. "I thank but you eat cookie. I brought for you. Is good."

Ike ate the rest of the cookie with satisfaction. Now he'd certainly been a bit nicer. Cousin Jake seemed to taste Ike's enjoyment. But Ike still didn't like to practice reading Hebrew with him.

That afternoon at the hospital ship, Ike shouted from his side of the pier to tell Papa all about the week's happenings and about the day he'd saved Boy. He told him about the seven surprises Mama's grandmother in Russia predicted, and counted five, so far: One—being allowed to keep Boy, two—Jake's arrival, three —surprising Papa at the ship, four—bringing Papa the gift of hope, and five—Cousin Jake's job at the bakery.

Then he gave Shirley the sweet roll from Jake to hand to Papa. Papa ate it and smacked his lips with enjoyment. He really seemed stronger as he listened to Ike chant and recite perfectly.

"You have prepared your speech, Ikey?" Papa asked.

"Yes, Papa," Ike said.

"On Thursday you will no longer be a boy. You will be a Jewish man, Ikey. That's the meaning of Bar Mitzvah. You understand that? You will have responsibilities." Papa stopped talking so he could cough. Then catching his breath, he went on. "You will be expected to do justly, to love mercy, and to walk humbly with our God. My thoughts will be with you. My heart will be there. You must remember that. I wish I could be with you. I wish I had a present to give you but . . ."

Ike could see Papa wouldn't possibly be

well enough to come away from the hospital ship for the Bar Mitzvah. Even a visit to shul with the trip there and back, would be too much for him. Ike wanted to feel excited about his big day, but all he felt was sadness as he threw a kiss to Papa and walked to the train. Shirley looked as if she might cry any minute as she wheeled Papa back to Bellevue Hospital.

That night, after Ike got into bed, he tossed and turned restlessly. Mama must have heard him. She peeked in at Ike and covered him like she used to do when he was little, pushing the quilt up under his chin.

"Mama," he whispered.

"Oy, Ikey. You are getting nervous for your Bar Mitzvah? So what else is new?" She tried to cheer him. "Even Morton Weinstein was nervous for his."

"Sit down, Mama," Ike said, making room for her to sit beside him. She pulled the belt of her faded plain robe tighter, pushed her long night braid over her shoulder, and sat down. "I've been thinking." Ike spoke softly.

"Of what?" Mama asked, and stroked his

forehead as if that would clear his thoughts and calm him.

"I've been thinking about what it means to become a man."

"Yes?" Mama waited for Ike to go on.

"I think," Ike spoke slowly, "that becoming a man means accepting that all my wishes and dreams won't come true—accepting that Papa won't be with me on my Bar Mitzvah day."

Mama kissed his forehead and smiled at him—just a faint smile.

Why did she smile at words like that? Sad words it seemed to Ike. She probably just thought it was cute that he was growing up. Mamas are like that, he figured.

Mama was filled with joy that Wednesday before the big day, or was she pretending in order to take Ike's mind off missing Papa? After Jake set off for work, she bustled about the kitchen as if everything was just perfect. Mrs. Weinstein came down to help and to worry about if there would be enough food, what to wear, when to leave for the Bar Mitzvah.

Mama just hummed and pulled out her big iron, deep-frying pan. Next she took out eggs and yeast, a dish of butter, and a sack of flour.

"Aren't you worried?" Mrs. Weinstein asked.

"As long as you're going to worry," Mama shrugged her shoulders as she spoke, "so I won't worry. Why should we both be upset?"

"Eva, I could plotz from you," Mrs. Weinstein said. "It's eight o'clock already and you haven't even started the cake. All night you bake? Like Jake at the bakery?"

"I bake . . . whenever," Mama answered.

Mama had no recipe for the yeast cake. She just took a handful or two of sugar and three cups of flour, a dash of salt, three eggs, some water, and yeast. She mixed and mixed the heavy mixture in a big bowl, saying, "Boychik, get out from under my feet, the oven is hot. You don't want to be a hot dog." And, "Bessie, darling, you are buzzing and flitting around." Then to Mrs. Weinstein she added, "Trying to work with Bessie around is like trying to eat with a fly buzzing around your head."

"Let me put the raisins in," Bessie begged, "and the nuts."

"Okay, Bessie, put, put already, you are making me nuts," Mama said.

Next Mama let Bessie taste the batter, wiping her finger across the mixing spoon and waiting for her smile of approval after Bessie licked the sweet mixture. Mrs. Weinstein went next and finally Mama herself gave the taste test.

Then Mama poured the mixture into the heavy frying pan that she used as a baking dish. After covering the pan with a clean, damp cloth and waiting for the dough to rise, she removed the cloth and sprinkled crumbs on top of the swollen dough. Next she placed the pan in the already heated oven of the black coal stove, as she said to Bessie, "Now go get me the dress you will wear tomorrow morning to Ike's Bar Mitzvah."

"Which dress, Mama?" Bessie liked to tease Mama with this make-believe idea of owning many dresses. And she loved when Mama would tease her back saying, "The golden one —with the diamonds on it." Mama gave her usual reply. For in reality Bessie had only one good dress and it was quite plain pink cotton. Soon Bessie clunked back into the kitchen wearing tin cans on her feet, pretending they were high-heeled, high-button shoes. Mama and Mrs. Weinstein laughed.

Ike found it difficult to go over his speech with all the noise going on around him and with the overpowering, wonderful, sweet smell of the yeast cake making his mouth water. He decided to save a big piece of cake for Papa. Tonight Papa was very much in his mind. A sad, empty feeling made waves inside him.

Then Mama interrupted his thoughts and called from the kitchen, "Ike, the light is flickering. Borrow a quarter from Mrs. Mantussi and put it in the gas meter." In each apartment on East 136th Street in the Bronx, there was a meter on the wall into which a quarter was deposited to pay for the gas used. Ike peered in the kitchen at the Welsbach mantle—a lacelike hood over the flickering gas flame, which gave light to the lamp hanging over the kitchen table. What a time to run out of gas, he thought, knowing what the flickering meant. If there was no money deposited in the meter, there would be no gas. And he still had to take a bath in the big, metal tub Mama would set up in the kitchen. After scouring it clean with ashes saved from the coal stove and kept in a tin pan till needed, she would fill the tub with water heated on the stove. Ike would then have to scrub himself good and clean with brown Octagon soap, and yell to everyone to keep out of the kitchen.

"Ike, go get the quarter already. The light is out altogether now," Mama said.

Ike raced downstairs, but Mrs. Mantussi had no money to spare this week, so Ike went to the Murphy's.

"Hey, Murph," Ike said, "you got a quarter for the gas meter?"

"Yeah," Patrick Murphy said. "My old man just got a tip when he made a delivery."

"Thanks," Ike said, taking the quarter.

"We'll owe you; when your light flickers let me know."

Ike returned to his apartment and triumphantly deposited a quarter in the wall meter. Bessie clapped her hands as the lights went on again.

Then, finally, when the kitchen was all his, Ike bathed. The warm water felt good but the scrubbing didn't.

Ike was glad to get out of the tub and into his bed. But he tossed about restlessly on this last night of his boyhood, telling himself over and over again, that at least Papa would be at Temple in his thoughts and heart. He tried hard to accept that. Finally, quite late, he fell asleep wondering if there would really be two more surprises before sundown tomorrow.

9
THE
BAR MITZVAH
SURPRISE

In Ike's neighborhood it was a tradition to have Bar Mitzvahs on Thursday mornings, early, so people wouldn't miss too much work.

This morning of November third, Ike stared into the bathroom mirror at his lathered face as he tried to shave the stubble on his chin. He'd soon have to shave every day, he thought.

A shudder ran through him as he worried that his changing voice might crack while he chanted, or that he might get a lump in his throat at the moment when Papa should have been having an aliyah.

Ike dressed in his blue serge suit and went into the kitchen. "Thank God it is a clear day." He heard Mama say to Jake.

Mama put both hands on Ike's cheeks, then kvelled, looking at him with this special look of pride. Then she brushed some lint from his shoulder and tugged at the sleeves as if that would lengthen them to cover Ike's summer of growing. With Papa sick, this year there'd been no money for a new suit, not even for this special occasion. Last, she smoothed his hair down with a drop of butter. Mama, Jake, and Bessie were dressed and busy talking, as if they'd been ready, for a while. Jake rubbed his eyes, sleepy from his night's work. Ike couldn't figure out what was going on—something mysterious. But there was no time to ask questions now.

When everyone was ready, including Boy, whom Bessie had insisted upon dressing up with a blue ribbon around his neck, Mama wrapped up the yeast cake and announced her plan. Jake, too, carried a package. Ike wondered what was in it.

"We are going to the pier, Ikey, to the hospital ship before it leaves for the day, so Papa can at least see how you look all dressed up on this special day. Mr. Murphy is taking us in the furniture delivery truck. So now, we go!" Mama said.

Everything was happening so fast. Ike felt like weeds were growing in his stomach—a terrible nervous feeling mixed with excitement as everyone piled into the truck and rode to the pier, arriving as the sun rose fully and brightly in the sky above the rippling water.

Ike couldn't believe his eyes when he got there. For waiting on the pier was a crowd of people . . . and he knew them all. There was the East 136th Street army of boys and their parents. There was Murray the newsman. There was Rosie, Arnold, and Baby Murray, dressed up in a little sailor jacket, and there was the rabbi from cheder. There was a table set up with food on it, herrings, potatoes, peppers, corn bread, rolls, and wine. In the center of this Mama placed the yeast cake. But there, best of all, off in the distance but close enough to see and hear—were Shirley, the nurse, and Papa.

Ike waved to them all. Another good surprise! The sixth, he figured to himself, his heart pounding with excitement.

Now Mama looked at him and said, "Remember when you told me how becoming a man means accepting that wishes and dreams won't come true?" She gently touched his shoulders and went on, "This surprise is my gift to you today, Ikey dear, to show you that sometimes even when you are a man—sometimes even when you don't expect it—your wishes and dreams will come true." Mama moved her fingers to stroke Ike's chin as she spoke. "You must never give up wishing and dreaming—that part of being a child gives you the strength to be a man. And if I could make for Rosie and Arnold a block wedding, why not for you a Bar Mitzvah outside?"

"How did you arrange it all, Mama?" Ike asked.

Mama waited for the horn blast of a passing tugboat to quiet. "I visited the rabbi at cheder and he said any place where ten Jewish men—a *minyan*—gather, God is there. So," she pointed to the guests, "we have here today more than ten Jewish men and the rabbi brought with him the ancient scroll, the sacred Torah. If Papa couldn't come to your Bar Mitzvah, then your Bar Mitzvah, Ikey, just had to come to Papa, and that's that!" A river breeze blew and Mama took a deep breath of the fresh air, then continued. "I telephoned to Papa's doctor and to Shirley and they both agreed this surprise for Papa would cheer him. He is getting better, although he will not be home for a while, and it will be even longer until he can work.

"So now—" Mama announced in a loud voice, "let the Bar Mitzvah begin!" The rabbi set up a raised platform on some wood planks from the pier and placed on it a cloth-covered reading desk to hold the ark in which the Torah was protected. Mama pinched Ike's cheeks and kissed his head then placed upon his curly hair a satin yarmulke she'd carried in her pocketbook. Jake took out the package he'd been carrying, opened it, and placed on Ike's shoulders a tallis—a prayer shawl with 613 fringes for the 613 mitzvot in the Bible, a tallis with one blue thread in each corner because it is commanded in the Bible.

"I brought this from the old country," Jake said, and placed his small hand on Ike's shoulder. "You will do good job. I teach, teach, teach. You ready now."

And Ike did feel ready now. Ready to think like a man. Maybe even to see the good in Cousin Jake—to see that he'd made Ike study hard so he would be ready.

This time Ike didn't push Jake's hand away. He patted it and felt love for this man who wasn't taking Papa's place but was just adding a place of his own in Ike's heart. Yes, Jake's arrival had turned out to be a good surprise after all. Perhaps, Ike thought, you don't always know right away what might turn out to be good or bad.

Ike felt like a Jewish man when Cousin Jake helped him put on tefillin. One box Ike placed on the inner side of his left arm just above the elbow. "This places it next to the heart when you pray," Jake explained. Then he had Ike coil the strap around the left forearm exactly seven times.

The other box Jake placed in the middle of Ike's forehead, high up above the hairline. Then the strap was looped around the head and knotted. As he had been shown by Jake and as he'd seen Papa often do, Ike fixed the two ends of the straps so they joined over the shoulder and were brought forward. Then Ike wound the arm band strap around his middle finger three times.

"With the donning of tefillin the everyday things are removed and the prayer's mind is devoted to truth and righteousness," the rabbi explained.

Mama took Bessie by the hand and moved toward Shirley who was at the side of the table where all the women gathered. They were observing the religious ritual of keeping the required separation from the men to avoid any distractions from praying.

The morning service began and Ike was

proud when the rabbi asked Jake to lead the congregation in chanting a portion. Ike waited nervously, shifting his weight from one big foot to the other—waiting for his turn to read.

Finally, the rabbi called him up to the bema, the raised platform. The Torah was now out of the ark. Then Ike listened for the voice he'd been longing to hear. Tears came to his eyes as Papa, a yarmulke on his head, chanted the ancient Hebrew blessing. And his voice, for the first time, grew stronger rather than weaker with each word. He even held up both hands and reached outward, as if to feel closer to Ike and his family and friends. Everyone watched Papa.

Next in a loud clear voice Ike chanted the Torah portion—the beginning segment about Noah. Even the rabbi complimented him, then and there.

Ike felt proud when the rabbi himself referred to Papa and Cousin Jake as very learned men, and to Ike as a good reader.

Then it was time for Ike's speech. He stood up tall, the river breeze blowing through his hair. He faced the rows of standing people, glancing at the front row where the East 136th Street army of boys made encouraging gestures. He cleared his throat. Then taking a deep breath of the fresh air, he spoke.

"My dear beloved parents, sister, relatives, and friends. It is a great honor and privilege for me to be able to talk to all of you"—and he looked right at Papa—"on my thirteenth birthday.

"I want to thank my father and mother, my sister, the rabbi and congregation, all my friends including some special new ones—my cousin Jake, Shirley, and Boy. Today I feel as happy as Noah must have felt when the flood waters receded. Today is my first day as a Jewish man. I am now responsible for the mitzvot —the commandments. Now I can be a tenth in a minyan and I am proud of it. I promise to do justly, to love mercy, and to walk humbly with my God . . . and I also promise to make my parents proud of me."

Then, just before it was time for the scroll to be put back in the ark, Ike joined the rabbi and the elders of the congregation as they marched the scroll around. Then the men and boys kissed the fringes of their prayer shawls and touched those fringes to the scroll in respect for the Torah.

And then came the moment the boys waited for, the moment when they got to throw little tied-up gauze bags filled with sour balls, chocolates, nuts, and raisins, and wish everyone a *zessen yahr*—a good year. Both Bessie and Boy raced to get the bags of treats.

There was much hugging and congratulating and patting on the back. "Mazel tov!" Ike heard and felt it all as if in a daze. Then he saw Papa waving to get his attention and Ike quieted everyone down so he could hear Papa's words.

"I have for you a present after all, Ikey," Papa said. "I thought and thought. I wanted to give you something you would always remember. Not germs, so only Shirley has done the handling," Papa even joked.

A surprise gift from Papa. *The seventh surprise,* Ike thought to himself.

"I have here for you," Papa said, pointing to a pile next to his wheelchair, "these sticks that Shirley gathered for me. Give them to Ikey," Papa instructed. "Just half of the pile. Give them to Ikey one by one. And as Shirley gives them to you for me, Ikey, try to break them one by one."

That would be easy, Ike thought, taking each heavy stick and snapping it in half, wondering what Papa was up to.

Everyone watched Ike and listened to Papa except Boy who was chewing on one of the sticks Ike had dropped onto the wooden pier. He pushed part of it through the boards and looked sideways with surprise at the sound of the splash of water.

"Now," Papa said to Shirley, "give Ikey the other six sticks. Hold these as if they are one and try to break them."

Ike took the bundle of sticks from Shirley. A breeze stirred the water and made it slap against the pier. Bessie twirled around and Mama took hold of her little hand so she wouldn't twirl off the pier.

Then Ike tried with all his might to break the bundle of sticks. He was a man now. He figured he should be able to—that perhaps Papa expected him to be able to be strong enough to break the bundle of sticks.

At a signal from Sammy and Dave the rest of the boys chorused, "You can do it, Ike, you can do it." And Boy barked an encouraging bark.

"You're turning red, Ike," Mr. Mantussi called out.

"Be careful, Ike. You don't want to strain and get a hernia, a killer." Mrs. Weinstein chuckled.

Ike tried and tried but he could not break the sticks when held as one. He slowly looked up at Papa.

Instead of being disappointed Papa looked proud. "Ikey, those sticks represent members of a family. Alone, each can be broken, but when a family stays together—it cannot. That is my present for you, Ikey, my son. To remember that and my love always. Now when do we eat?" Papa laughed. "Mama told me she was baking her yeast cake—that will make me better for sure."

So after the rabbi nodded approval at Papa for passing to the next generation stories of tradition, and blessed the food, everybody had a something to eat. Rosie and Arnold from uptown had provided the herring and corn bread treats. But Ike had everything he wanted— seven good surprises; a delicious slice of Mama's yeast cake melting in his mouth; Papa feeling better; Mama, Bessie, and Cousin Jake all close by; and Shirley in his sight petting Boy. It felt good to be a man, he decided, especially in a family that sticks together, yet!